IN THE DOGHOUSE WITH THE POLICE...
AGAIN

"Mrs. Doolittle," Mallory repeated, raising bushy eyebrows in mock surprise, "perhaps you'd care to explain why you are at the scene of this particular crime?"

"It's a long story," I said, thinking that the telling was not going to do much to alter his previous opinion of me as an interfering pet detective who didn't know enough to stay out of trouble.

"I have plenty of time," he said.

"Well," I began. "I found this cat in a trap this morning..."

"Aha! What did I say? Animals again."

Infuriating man. I ignored the remark, and said, "Don't you think it odd that..."

"Don't start with your animal theories again," he warned. "The oddest thing about the case so far, Mrs. Doolittle, is that you're on the scene."

MORE MYSTERIES FROM THE
BERKLEY PUBLISHING GROUP...

DOG LOVERS' MYSTERIES STARRING HOLLY WINTER: With her Alaskan malamute Rowdy, Holly dogs the trails of dangerous criminals. "A gifted and original writer."—Carolyn G. Hart

by Susan Conant

A NEW LEASH ON DEATH	A BITE OF DEATH
DEAD AND DOGGONE	PAWS BEFORE DYING

DOG LOVERS' MYSTERIES STARRING JACKIE WALSH: She's starting a new life with her son and an ex-police dog named Jake . . . teaching film classes and solving crimes!

by Melissa Cleary

A TAIL OF TWO MURDERS	FIRST PEDIGREE MURDER	THE MALTESE PUPPY
DOG COLLAR CRIME	SKULL AND DOG BONES	MURDER MOST BEASTLY
HOUNDED TO DEATH	DEAD AND BURIED	OLD DOGS
AND YOUR LITTLE DOG, TOO		

SAMANTHA HOLT MYSTERIES: Dogs, cats, and crooks are all part of a day's work for this veterinary technician . . . "Delightful!"—Melissa Cleary

by Karen Ann Wilson

EIGHT DOGS FLYING	COPY CAT CRIMES
BEWARE SLEEPING DOGS	CIRCLE OF WOLVES

CHARLOTTE GRAHAM MYSTERIES: She's an actress with a flair for dramatics—and an eye for detection. "You'll get hooked on Charlotte Graham!"—*Rave Reviews*

by Stefanie Matteson

MURDER AT THE SPA	MURDER ON THE SILK ROAD	MURDER AMONG THE ANGELS
MURDER AT TEATIME	MURDER AT THE FALLS	MURDER UNDER THE PALMS
MURDER ON THE CLIFF	MURDER ON HIGH	

PEACHES DANN MYSTERIES: Peaches has never had a very good memory. But she's learned to cope with it over the years . . . Fortunately, though, when it comes to murder, this absentminded amateur sleuth doesn't forgive and forget!

by Elizabeth Daniels Squire

WHO KILLED WHAT'S-HER-NAME?	WHOSE DEATH IS IT ANYWAY?
MEMORY CAN BE MURDER	IS THERE A DEAD MAN IN THE HOUSE?
REMEMBER THE ALIBI	

HEMLOCK FALLS MYSTERIES: The Quilliam sisters combine their culinary and business skills to run an inn in upstate New York. But when it comes to murder, their talent for detection takes over . . .

by Claudia Bishop

A TASTE FOR MURDER	A DASH OF DEATH	DEATH DINES OUT
A PINCH OF POISON	MURDER WELL-DONE	

Delilah Doolittle
AND THE
Motley Mutts

Patricia Guiver

BERKLEY PRIME CRIME, NEW YORK

DELILAH DOOLITTLE AND THE MOTLEY MUTTS

A Berkley Prime Crime Book / published by arrangement with the author

PRINTING HISTORY
Berkley Prime Crime edition / April 1998

All rights reserved.
Copyright © 1998 by Patricia Guiver.
This book may not be reproduced in whole or in part, by mimeograph or any other means, without permission.
For information address: The Berkley Publishing Group, a member of Penguin Putnam Inc.,
200 Madison Avenue, New York, NY 10016.

The Penguin Putnam Inc. World Wide Web site address is
http://www.penguinputnam.com

ISBN: 0-425-16266-4

Berkley Prime Crime Books are published
by The Berkley Publishing Group,
a member of Penguin Putnam Inc.,
200 Madison Avenue, New York, NY 10016.
The name BERKLEY PRIME CRIME and the BERKLEY PRIME CRIME
design are trademarks belonging to Berkley Publishing Corporation.

PRINTED IN THE UNITED STATES OF AMERICA

10 9 8 7 6 5 4 3 2 1

Acknowledgments

My thanks to Dr. Victoria Valdez of the All Cat Veterinary Clinic for her advice on the treatment of cat injuries; and to Mark McDorman, Chief of Field Operations for Orange County Animal Control, for the information on trapping. If I got anything wrong, it's through no fault of theirs.

And, as always, thanks to my own special support group: friends Donna Calkin and Patricia McFall, my agent Patricia Teal, and my many colleagues in the animal welfare field who inspire me with their dedication.

To Mariya, beloved pet of Donna and Gene.

and

To Buddy, a wirehaired fox terrier, the first of many wonderful canine companions to share my life.

"To a man the greatest blessing is individual liberty; to a dog it is the last word in despair."

—William Lyon Phelps

· 1 ·
Watson Is Missing

"WATSON!"

I awoke with a start, dreaming I had heard her barking. My toes reached down to the end of the bed to touch her comforting Doberman bulk.

She wasn't there.

I'd heard her get up during the night and had drifted back to sleep, listening for the flap of the doggie door signalling her return.

She couldn't still be outside. On these damp November nights she'd hurry back in just as soon as she was through watering her horse, as the saying goes. She was putting on weight. Maybe she'd got stuck in the doggie door again.

I swung my legs over the edge of the bed, feet groping for slippers. The clock on the nightstand indicated half past five.

She wasn't in the kitchen or in her favourite chair. I went to the back door and called softly.

"Watson."

It was still dark outside, the yard shrouded in heavy

fog, typical of early winter in southern California, particularly this close to the beach.

"Watson!" I called again, louder this time. Was it my imagination, or did I hear a distant answering bark?

I got dressed, hastily pulling grey sweatpants and hooded sweatshirt over my cosy Lanz nightgown. Then tennis shoes and socks. I stuffed my uncombed, fading chestnut locks under a cap and tucked a flash-light in my pocket.

Worried though I was, the irony of the situation did not escape me. Delilah Doolittle, pet detective, out looking for her own dog. I was glad my only observer was an opossum scurrying along the neighbour's fence, babies clinging perilously to her back.

I brought my professional expertise to bear on the situation.

There were really only two directions Watson might have taken. Down the street, across the Pacific Coast Highway to the beach, a favourite spot for "walkies", or through a hole in the back hedge, over the footbridge across the flood control channel, to the Surf City wetlands.

The opossum gave me an idea. Maybe during her nocturnal wanderings Watson had caught a scent that awakened long dormant instincts and had answered the call of the wild.

I followed my own instincts and headed for the wetlands.

I continued calling, softly at first while still within

earshot of the neighbours, louder as I crossed the bridge to the loop trail used by the bird-watchers and eco-tourists who came to view the ducks, herons, pelicans, egrets, and other waterfowl who regard the salt marsh as their personal Motel 6 on the Pacific flyway.

Dense, drenching fog, cool on my cheeks, prevented me from seeing more than a few feet ahead. Droplets hung on the brim of my cap and my eyelashes.

I called again, louder now. Startled, a heron rose out of the cordgrass, flapping away through the mist like a pterodactyl rising from the primeval ooze.

I listened for another bark, but all I could hear was the rushing of the ocean tide a few hundred yards away and the faint, mournful moan of a foghorn.

Up ahead, the footpath took a sharp incline onto firmer ground and looped around a bunker, a relic of coastal artillery defense from World War II. Maybe Watson had taken refuge there for some reason. Continuing to call, I pressed on.

Moments later, I was rewarded with an answering bark. At almost the same time, the elongated dome-like shape of the concrete, earth-covered bunker came into view.

"Okay girl, I'm coming," I called.

Watson covered the few remaining feet between us and uttered a low-pitched bark, as if trying to tell me something.

"You naughty thing, bringing me out here like this. I'm drenched," I scolded lightly, relieved that she was safe. "Come along. Let's go home."

But she turned and trotted away from me, looking over her shoulder to make sure I was following.

I rounded the rear of the bunker and there, a few feet away, I saw the trap.

· 2 ·

A Deadly Discovery

A SMALL ANIMAL struggled to free its rear leg from the vicious, steel-jawed trap. It was Watson's friend Hobo, the itinerant ginger tom who occasionally ventured into our kitchen through the doggie door. Watson, not always the most tolerant of creatures, had surprised me by not chasing him off.

At my approach, Hobo renewed his struggles, no doubt suspecting that I was the bearer of fresh torment. An angry, terrified feral cat is not something one approaches lightly. But I had to act quickly. Putting aside my fears, I set about unspringing the trap, first removing my sweatshirt and gently placing it around the cat. I was taking no chances. The scratch of a feral cat and the resulting infection were not something I was anxious to experience.

Compressing the springs to release the tension on the jaws, I spread them apart and gently pulled the cat free. He was weak from shock and loss of blood. Wrapping the sweatshirt more tightly around him to prevent his escape, I carried him back to the house,

Watson trotting along beside me, jumping up occasionally to see what was happening to her friend.

Not stopping to dress properly, I grabbed another sweatshirt and headed for the vet.

THE SIGN HANGING from the beak of the carved wooden pelican announced Wellington Scott, DVM. Dr. Willie, as he was known to his friends, lived on the beach side of the Pacific Coast Highway, and his office and his home were one. Usually at this hour he would be surfing, but I was in luck. The fog had kept him indoors this morning.

He didn't so much as raise an eyebrow at my getup, though I must have looked far from the proper, middle-aged English lady I like to consider myself.

The vet didn't look much like the conventional doctor, come to that. In his mid-thirties, wearing a dark purple wet suit, his black hair tied in a ponytail, olive complexioned, a silver hoop adorning one ear, he looked more like a latter-day pirate than the competent vet I knew him to be. An aquiline nose kept him from being film-star handsome. He was, nevertheless, considered quite a hunk by the local female population. In my day, we'd have called him "a bit of all right".

At six feet plus, he towered over my five-foot-one-inch frame as he took Hobo from my arms and went about treating him for shock, setting up IV lines and examining the wound.

I spoke the concern uppermost in my mind: "Will he have to be put to sleep?"

"I doubt it," he said as he carefully checked the cat over. "Let's give him a couple of days to stabilize. He's lost a lot of blood, and he'll need a transfusion. We may not be able to save the leg. But he'll be okay. He looks like a tough old guy."

He made some notes in his file. "This is the third one I've seen in three weeks," he continued. "A client brought in her Collie just the other day. Managed to save his leg, though. But I'm advising everyone to keep their pets close to home."

"I thought we were leaving predator control to the coyotes," I said. "I haven't heard of any special trap permits being issued lately."

Coyotes prey on the foxes, feral cats, and other creatures which can quickly decimate endangered bird populations, particularly the light-footed clapper rail that unwisely chooses to nest in the cordgrass.

Tears filled my eyes, whether with compassion for the cat or anger at whoever had set the trap, I wasn't sure. But one thing I was sure of. Someone had to put a stop to the trapping.

"I'm going to see Bill about this," I said, reaching a sudden decision. "Maybe I can catch him before he leaves for work. That way I can have a few words with him in private."

Bill Jackson was a biologist employed by the city parks and recreation department to supervise the wet-

lands. He and his wife Rosemary were old friends of
mine.

IT WAS NEARLY eight o'clock, and the fog was beginning to lift by the time I reached their house, a
modest ranch-style a couple of blocks away from my
home.

I parked my station wagon in the driveway. Leaving Watson in the car, I marched to the front door,
knocking louder than is my habit, then, getting no
response, leaning on the doorbell in frustration.

Still no answer. I knocked again, harder this time.
The door swung open a little, and I pushed it a bit
farther.

"Hallo?" I called, venturing into the small hall-
way. "Bill. Rosemary. Anyone home?"

From the kitchen came the sound of a television
morning news program.

"Hallo?" I said again, walking into the kitchen.
"I'm sorry to barge in, but no one seemed to hear my
knock, and it's important . . ."

But not important enough to get Bill's attention.

He was lying faceup on the white ceramic tile floor,
a fair-size kitchen knife stuck in his chest.

❧ 3 ❧
With Friends Like These

"WHY IS IT, Mrs. Doolittle," Detective Mallory of the Surf City Police Department was saying, "that whenever I have a homicide case with the remotest connection to animals, you are the first on the scene?"

The coincidence had not escaped me. "Somebody has to be," was all I ventured.

It was a couple of months since I had last seen Jack Mallory. I had forgotten how attractive he was. About five-foot-ten, a little on the heavy side, but comfortable. His thick grey hair, curling around the ears, was rendered unruly by his habit of running his hand through it when he was puzzled or exasperated—as often seemed to be the case whenever I was around. In well-cut tweed jacket and tan corduroy slacks, tan shirt, and brown checked tie, he put one more in mind of an absent-minded professor than an astute police-man, though the penetrating blue-grey eyes warned one not to try to put anything over on him.

We were in the Jacksons' living room, where I had waited after dialling 911, not wanting to linger over the gruesome scene a moment longer than necessary. Bill's blood on the hitherto spotless white tile floor; the overturned wood block knife holder, the spilled knives; the mindless chatter of a television weatherman a surreal accompaniment, were images I would not soon forget.

"Mrs. Doolittle," Mallory repeated, raising bushy eyebrows in mock surprise, "perhaps you'd care to explain why you are at the scene of this particular crime?"

"It's a long story," I said, thinking that the telling was not going to do much to alter his previous opinion of me as an interfering pet detective who didn't know enough to stay out of trouble.

"I have plenty of time," he said.

"Well," I began, "I found this cat in a trap this morning . . ."

"Aha! What did I say. Animals again."

Infuriating man. I ignored the remark and said, "Don't you think it odd that . . ."

"Don't start with your animal theories again," he warned. "The oddest thing about the case so far, Mrs. Doolittle, is that you're on the scene."

I continued my train of thought. "I think it's strange that there's no sign of Bill's wife, Rosemary. She works nights at St. Mary's hospital. She should be home by now." I feared for her safety. The police had already searched the house. Both cars were still in the garage.

"We've put out an APB on her," he said. "It doesn't appear to be a burglary; nothing's been disturbed. But only she can tell us if anything's missing." He looked serious. "When we find her, she's got some explaining to do."

Slowly it dawned on me what he was thinking.

"Surely you don't suspect Rosemary," I said, aghast.

"At this point, everybody's a suspect, including you," he said. "But it's the typical MO of the outraged or battered wife, grabbing the closest weapon available, in this case a kitchen knife."

"Outraged and battered, nonsense," I said stiffly. "Please don't waste valuable time on that theory. Rosemary may be in danger right now, kidnapped, murdered. We have to find her."

"You're not including yourself in that 'we', I hope," he replied. "Leave the investigating to us. We are well aware of the potential dangers to Mrs. Jackson. I suggest you stay out of trouble yourself, and stick to chasing stray dogs."

If that remark was intended to get my dander up, he had succeeded. Fortunately for my decorum, however, the interview was interrupted by the entrance of Police Officer Bill Offley, a man who truly fit the description of "flatfoot". Tall, heavily built, he seemed to have more body than he knew what to do with. A graceless oaf, I had labeled him in our previous encounters. He didn't think much of me, either, if his occasional smart-aleck references to me as "the pet dick" were anything to go by. There had certainly been no love lost between us during our encounter in the Lomax case in which it had been my misfortune to be involved the previous September.

"Excuse me, sir," he said now, his lugubrious expression taking in my presence with disapproval. "There's a woman here, claims to have information about the wife."

Mallory's "I'll see her in a minute, when I'm through with Mrs. Doolittle," was cut short by a shrill "Delilah Doolittle! What in the world are you doing here?" uttered in an unmistakable Yorkshire accent as a thin, middle-aged woman entered the room. Dressed in bright green sweatpants and a purple top, spiky grey hair poking out strawlike from under a red knit cap, she carried a clipboard overloaded with sheets of paper, some of which fluttered to the ground as she pushed past Offley in a manner that brooked no denial.

"Give over, lad," she said as Offley tried to bar the way. " 'A woman' indeed. Tha' knows me well enough."

That was Mabel Redpath's way. Always implying a familiarity where more than likely none existed.

Much to my annoyance, she was the same with me. Though I was reluctant to acknowledge any such relationship, she took it for granted that our mutual British heritage conferred automatic kinship. Apart from a shared concern for animals, we had absolutely nothing in common, and I found her pushy manners vulgar and offensive. I had been holding her at bay for years. Although my sympathies often lay with her animal rights causes, she had never yet been able to enlist my participation in any of her well-intentioned but frequently ill-advised sorties. She had once led a hapless band of followers onto the firing range of a local military base, on the strength of a rumour that the habitat of the endangered kangeroo rat was about to be destroyed. They had barely escaped with their lives.

Poor Mabel. Her heart was in the right place, but she went about it all wrong.

"Still doing your pet detecting, Delilah? I hear you showed up that German shepherd breeder good and proper. The hell with all breeders, I say. All dogs should be fixed. Pigs, too," she added, throwing a defiant stare in Offley's direction. They'd had more than one run-in, though Mabel had yet to achieve her ultimate goal: arrest, martyrdom, and the six o'clock news.

Mallory indicated to Offley to let her stay.

"You have some information?" he asked her coldly.

Mabel took a sheet from the clipboard, dropping several more as she did so, and said, "Mabel Redpath. I'm the Neighborhood Watch block captain, and I have some observations to report."

I could well believe it. She was a regular nosey

parker, always ready to back her nose in other people's business.

"I live two houses down," she was saying. "There's been some very funny goings-on around here lately. It's that Rosemary Jackson. Coming home at all hours of the night. And then early this morning, when I went to call in me moggies, I saw her leave the house with a suitcase. She got into a taxi."

"Did you notice what company it was?" asked Mallory.

"Ee by gum, it were that foggy, it was hard to tell. It was a yellowish colour, I think. Though it might have been an optical delusion." Mallory hid a grin at the absurd malapropism.

He stood up. "Thank you, er," looking at his notebook, "Mrs. Redpath. Please give the officer your full name and address, and we'll be along to get your statement a little later."

"Oh, 'e knows where I live, don't you Billy-boy," she said, giving Offley a friendly nudge.

Billy-boy's jowly face turned crimson as, spluttering, he escorted her out.

She nodded good-bye to me. "Stay in touch, Delilah. I'll see you at the Coastal Commission meeting tomorrow."

Thrusting a flyer into my hand, she left, tarrying by the kitchen door long enough to take in all she could as she went.

Mallory watched her leave, then turned back to me. "Friend of yours?" he smiled.

He could hardly be blamed for thinking so. My outfit alone put us in the same category. Too late, I realized what a sight I must present. Unwashed, uncombed, an old sweatshirt over barely concealed nightgown. Tennis shoes covered with mud.

I sighed. It seemed it was my lot in life to be misunderstood by Detective Jack Mallory.

. 4 .

Wildlife Rebellion

"WE'RE STAYING AT the BBC," Evie Cavendish's upper-class English accent came wafting out of the answering machine. I had to think for a minute. To me, BBC could only mean the British Broadcasting Corporation, but I hadn't heard that Auntie Beebe was taking in boarders.

Returning home from my distressing visit to the Jacksons', I had found more than the usual number of messages on my machine.

Evie's was the first. The gist of it being that her husband Howard had recently been appointed to the California Coastal Commission, and they were in the area to attend a series of public hearings, the first of which was to be held in Surf City the following evening. They were staying at their apartment at the Beverly Bayside Club in Newport Beach and, of course, I was expected to drop everything and have lunch with them.

But what did I have to drop? It wasn't like I was overwhelmed with work. With only one case right now—a Puli who stubbornly refused to be found—business was alarmingly slow.

So why was I so reluctant to avail myself of an elegant lunch with my old school chum? I loved her dearly, but it was one of those relationships where distance lends enchantment. Up close and personal, she was hypercritical of everything about me: my house, my work, my lifestyle, and most of all my marital status—or lack thereof. Dear Evie. Ever since our youth when she had taken me under her wing at the posh private school I was attending on a scholarship, she has only wanted the best for me. In other words, A Really Nice Man, preferably someone like her beloved Howard: kind, attentive, and above all, wealthy. Nothing wrong with that, but I preferred to leave my fate to Random Chance.

I listened to the rest of the messages. My ad in the lost and found column generated a variety of animal-related calls, many of which had nothing whatever to do with pets, lost or found. It was as if a talent for finding lost pets implied an ability to solve any and all problems having to do with animals. I helped where I could, and word got around.

Today, there was more than the usual number of such calls. However, nothing approaching an assignment echoed forth. Instead, the machine offered a litany of distressed skunks, opossums, raccoons, and assorted other wildlife, their only crime being a desire to stay in the habitat which nature had intended for them.

Beep

"Do you know where I can get a humane trap for mice?" the woman asked. *"I don't want them hurt, just relocated."*

Even rodents have friends.

Beep

An older woman's voice querulously expressed concern about an opossum in her yard. *"I don't want to cause it any trouble, but I would like it to go away."*

I would call her back and tell her opossums were quite benign. Nature's janitors, in fact, ridding the yard of snails, fallen fruit, and other decaying matter.

Beep

Another skunk call. The city had been over-run with skunks lately, a natural consequence of a local development boom, of which my answering machine bore ample proof. What did people expect? They like their parks, but they want their nature sanitized. Certainly they want it deodorized.

This caller, claiming to represent SCUNKS (Stop Cruel and UnNecessary Killing of Skunks), was soliciting my help in starting an adopt-a-skunk campaign.

"A worthy but hopeless cause," I said to Watson, who was regarding me from the comfort of her well-worn armchair. "It's a wildlife rebellion. A sure sign the bulldozers are on the move."

Thinking of lost causes reminded me of Mabel's flyer. I extracted it from my pocket.

"SSCOWL," it was headed. "Save Surf City's Only Wetlands."

Mabel and the skunk savers must use the same copywriter. "Stop the bulldozers. Developers get tax dollars to build luxury homes for the wealthy. Attend showdown at the Coastal Commission meeting, City Hall, Tuesday night. Ask new commissioner Howard Cavendish how much he stands to profit from developing our precious wildlife habitat."

❀ 5 ❀
Lunch at the Club

"CHEERS, SWEETIE," SAID Evie, after the waitress had placed the three gin and tonics on the table. "Lovely to see you again."

I had joined my friend and her husband Howard for lunch in the elegant dining room of the Beverly Bayside Club. Outside, a storm raged with that unexpected intensity peculiar to southern California. The weatherman's prediction of sprinkles had, in reality, brought forth the kind of rain that caused mud slides on over-developed and fire-ravaged hillsides, flooding in the canyons, and headlines on the network news.

Every so often, a squall slapped rain-soaked white and yellow awnings against the windows. At the dock beyond, luxury motor yachts tossed restlessly at their moorings.

I was drenched by the time I arrived. Too embarrassed to hand over my ancient station wagon, replete with cat traps, pet-carriers, and other pet detective paraphernalia, to the parking valet, I had left it in the nether regions of the yacht club complex. Then, with my umbrella in danger of being turned inside out by sudden wind gusts, I had crossed the parking lot doing a fair Mary Poppins impersonation.

My hair, over which, in deference to Evie, I had taken considerable pains, now hung in limp strands. At her suggestion, I had attempted to cover the grey streaks with a bottle of something that delivered considerably less than the label promised, and I was rather afraid that the rain droplets now trickling down my cheeks might have taken on a brownish hue.

On greeting me in the lobby, Evie had stared at my hair in uncharacteristic silence, until I had felt compelled to offer a faltering explanation. Her response had been to gently dab at my face with a tissue, saying as she did so that she couldn't understand why anyone would want to make themselves look older than they need.

Why indeed? Clearly, tact was not a quality Evie had ever considered worth cultivating.

My tan wool pantsuit, partially covered by an old mackintosh which rarely saw the light of day except during infrequent visits to England, looked decidedly drab alongside Evie's smart outfit.

She and Howard were decked out in nearly identical nautical gear. Navy-blue blazers topped winter-white slacks, finely tailored, in Evie's case, to make the best of her well-rounded figure. Her red silk blouse was complemented by Howard's red polo-neck sweater. A jaunty navy-blue and white cap covered her expertly coloured ash blonde curls. A necklace of red, white, and blue beads tied the outfit together.

Over our spinach salad and poached salmon (Evie's choice; she was on a diet and we were expected to keep her company), we talked comfortably about familiar friends and brought each other up to date on our latest doings.

Our friendship has stood the test of time remarkably well despite the difference in our circumstances. After finishing school, we had come to America together in search of adventure, and had both married here. But there the similarities ended. Evie had married Howard, a wealthy Texan, and had, in her own words, been divinely happy ever since. I had met Roger at their wedding and had been immediately captivated by his ease in company, so different from my own inborn reticence. He was one of those people of whom it could truly be said that he never met a stranger. Life with Roger had done much to bring me out of myself, introducing me to new people and experiences, encouraging me to be less shy and inhibited. But his charm had eventually been his undoing; he had fallen in with the wrong crowd and had subsequently been killed in an accident in what, to this day, I continue to regard as questionable circumstances.

Though I might, on occasion, envy Evie her peace of mind from financial worries, I would not have traded with her. I was quite content with the life I had created for myself: the little house (all that Roger had left me), my job, and the company of my dear Watson satisfied all my needs.

Evie must have been reading my mind. "So, have you been seeing anyone?" she asked with lively interest. "Any marriage material in the offing?"

An honest and straightforward reply would have been that I had no wish to marry again, expressing the opinion that, present company excepted, husbands were an overrated commodity. Furthermore, that washing socks and cooking meals for an unappreciative male was not my idea of the most productive use of my time.

This ready retort eluded me, however. I merely shook my head, inevitably giving her the opening she'd no doubt been waiting for.

"Dee, you really are the limit," she exclaimed. "I have paraded before you a veritable army of eligible men: good-looking, well-off, and personable. You've turned up your nose at all of them. But you seem to have no hesitation in attaching yourself to a cadre of unsavoury misfits and eccentrics who, if not outright sponging off you, are taking up altogether too much of your time. Time, I might add, which would be better employed finding yourself a suitable husband."

To change the subject, I asked after their dogs, a surefire distraction. Chamois, their tiny Maltese, and Britt, a Brittany spaniel, both had been major players in the Lomax case.

"Britt's at home with Rosa," explained Evie. "She doesn't travel well."

"And Chamois?"

Evie put a well-manicured finger to her lips, then pointed under the table. Lifting the cloth, I saw a worn, brown leather sport bag. Through the partially opened zipper, I caught a glimpse of white fur. For Chamois, whose feet seldom touched the ground, the bag was his second home.

Evie took a sliver of salmon from her fork and slipped it under the table. "And what of your job?" she asked. "Still traipsing around dog pounds, looking for lost pets?" She managed to make my work sound like a particularly unpleasant habit.

I sighed. I should have seen that coming. She wasn't about to let me get away with anything.

"Well?" she prodded.

"Only one case at the moment. A Puli."

"A what? Never heard of it."

"Puli. Hungarian sheepdog. You must have seen them at Westminster. The ones with the dreadlocks. Medium size, black. Her name's Mariah, like the wind. And as far as I can tell, she's gone with. Absolutely no trace. Of course, it was over a week before the owner called me. To make matters worse, the dog's coming into heat soon. The owner's planning to breed her and doesn't want any accidental backyard liaisons."

"She should take better care of her then," snapped Evie. "Any ID?"

For all her superficial airs, Evie took pet ownership very seriously.

I shook my head. "Of course not," I said with heavy sarcasm. "If she'd been wearing a tag, she'd probably be back home by now."

If everyone put tags on their pets, I'd be out of business. Nothing would make me happier. Dealing with lost pets could be heart-breaking. Meanwhile, I would use my modest skills to reunite as many pets with their owners as I possibly could.

When we moved to a table in the bar for coffee and brandy, the conversation turned to the reason for their visit, the Coastal Commission meeting. Howard was a little apprehensive, this being his first public hearing. I told him I felt he would be fair and even-handed and assured him that his would be a voice of moderation in a situation rife with discord.

A thought occurred. "Here, what do you make of this?" I asked, showing him Mabel's flyer. "What does that mean, 'Ask Howard Cavendish how much he stands to profit'?"

It turned out that Howard did indeed own property adjacent to the northern boundary of the wetlands. If the area were developed, its value would increase dramatically.

"But I have no wish to exploit it," said Howard.

I believed him. He was so wealthy, one small parcel of land wouldn't affect him much one way or another. Besides, they were both genuinely concerned about preserving wildlife habitat, and he certainly had no desire to incur the wrath of Evie by running afoul of environmental issues.

Leaning over his shoulder, Evie regarded the flyer with disdain. "Of course we have no intention of profiting from this," she said. "We appreciate the importance of the wetlands quite as much as the next person. Poor little birds have to have somewhere to rest when they fly from the Arctic to South America or wherever. Though heaven knows why they can't just stay in one place where it's warm."

She took out a tiny gold cigarette lighter, inserted a Sobranie cigarette into a slender gold and diamond holder, and blew smoke away from the table.

Fingering the flyer, Howard appeared to hesitate for a moment. "How well do you know these people? Do you think they're the type to make threatening phone calls?"

I considered carefully. "No. I really don't. Mabel Redpath, she's their leader, is a little eccentric, truly dedicated to her causes, but she's not one to make personal threats. After all, she's British," I added with a smile. Then, "Have you called the police?"

At the mention of the police, Evie's eyes filled with concern.

Her reaction was not lost on Howard, and he hastily replied, "Well, I'm not taking it seriously. All part of the job. In this kind of situation, it's impossible to please everyone, and some are going to take it harder than others."

I had plenty of questions. What kind of threats? How many? A man or a woman's voice? But taking my cue from Howard, no more was said about the matter at that point. Neither of us wanted to worry Evie further. I would have to get Howard alone and ask him later.

That opportunity arose sooner than I expected. When Evie excused herself to go to the powder room, I immediately returned to the topic.

"Now, Howard. Tell me more about the phone calls."

"Like I said, Delilah, of course I'm concerned, but there's just something about them that sounds a bit half-baked, if you know what I mean."

"No, I don't. Tell me. What did they say?"

"Well, that's the stupid thing." Howard toyed with a cigar. "Simply that they knew who I was, why I was on the Commission, and that I should watch my step on the wetlands."

I seized on that. Watching one's step on the wetlands only meant one thing to me—watch out for steel-jawed traps!

"Was it a man's or a woman's voice?"

"Hard to tell. If you want the truth, it sounded like a woman trying to sound like a man."

I was beginning to have second thoughts about my protestations of Mabel's innocence. I wanted to ask Howard more, but Evie was making her elegant way back to the table.

I made a mental note to keep a close eye on Mabel from now on.

$\cdot$ 6 $\cdot$

Trouble Brewing

THE STORM CONTINUED into the evening, and a chill wind was blowing through the City Hall forecourt when I arrived for the Coastal Commission meeting.

Golden shafts of rain slanted in the lights illuminating the walkways. A small group of protesters huddled near the entrance, their home-made picket signs exhorting Save Surf City's Only Wetlands barely legible where the rain had caused the poster paint to run.

Mabel broke from the group and headed toward me.

"There you are, Delilah. I knew you wouldn't let us down," she said, thrusting a picket sign into my hands. She hurried off again without giving me a chance to decline.

Intent on divesting myself of the offending sign before Evie should catch sight of it, I looked around for a convenient dumping spot. Turning toward a nearby flower bed, I almost poked the sign into the eye of the man walking behind me. It was Detective Mallory. In the rain-dimmed twilight, I didn't recognized him at first. Wearing jeans and a navy-blue duffel coat, the hood pulled snug around his neck against the weather, he was out of what I had come to consider his uniform of well-tailored slacks and sports jacket.

He ducked, regarding the sign with amusement.

"Save Surf City's Onky Webloes," he read. "A newly discovered endangered species? I didn't know you counted activism among your hobbies, Mrs. Doolittle."

I looked at the rain-spattered sign in embarrassment. He seemed always to catch me at my worst.

"Actually, I'm here to support my friend, Howard Cavendish, one of the commissioners. How about you? Are you working crowd control?" I countered.

"No. Like yourself," he nodded at the sign, "I'm here as a concerned citizen."

I recalled that he, too, was a birder, and was about to take advantage of our mutual interest to pursue the conversation, when Mabel appeared again, tugging at my sleeve.

"Come along, luv. If tha' wants to speak, tha' has to take a number," she said, excitement broadening her north country accent.

Mallory turned abruptly and headed for the entrance, no doubt anxious to avoid any exchange with her. Mabel moved on to round up her supporters. I waited until she was out of sight, then tossed the sign aside and hurried in out of the rain.

The council chamber was packed. It was a recent

addition to Surf City's civic center, part of the renovation deemed necessary to enhance the city's new-found image as an upscale residential community. An image not entirely welcomed by long-time residents like myself, who preferred the casual, slightly shabby ambience of beach-side bungalows, surfers' shops, and fish taco stands. The auditorium, with its tiered, theatre-style seating, could be accessed from either the lower level, where I had entered, or from the upper level, from which city offices, the police station, and jail could also be reached.

I looked around. Anyone with an opinion on the future of the wetlands, from environmentalists to building contractors, seemed to be there, eager to voice their opinions to members of the California Coastal Commission, which had to review environmental impact reports and consider public input before approving plans for development.

Prominent among the local environmentalists was Amelia Mann, president of the local wetlands preservation society, who now waved to me, indicating a seat next to her. Impeccably dressed, as always, she was wearing a tailored navy-blue pantsuit, navy pumps, and a white and blue paisley scarf knotted around her throat, pinned in place with a silver brooch in the shape of a California least tern, an endangered bird that returned to Surf City every year to nest. Her dark brown hair shaped close to her head, Amelia looked the picture of a headmistress of a private girls' school, which she was.

"Did you hear about Bill Jackson?" she asked as soon as I sat down.

I nodded. I didn't feel up to telling her that I was the one who had discovered the body, dreading the inevitable quizzing that would result.

"Do you think it could have anything to do with this business?" she said, gesturing to take in the crowded auditorium.

"You mean development? What makes you say that?"

"Well, Bill never made a secret of his opposition to the project. Maybe he went too far, and somebody decided to silence him."

Any observations I might have made on that theory were cut short by the arrival of an acquaintance of Amelia's taking a seat on her other side. It was Bud Hefner, a World War II U.S. Army veteran and local hero who I knew by reputation but had never previously met. I understood he was something of a recluse, no doubt because of the jagged scars slanting across what might once have been a rather handsome face.

Amelia introduced us and, as he removed his hat, revealing closely trimmed iron-grey hair, and placed it in his lap, I asked what had brought him out on such a rough night.

He appeared to consider the question, merely intended as social chitchat, with more seriousness than it warranted, then responded in a deep, deliberate voice which, though well articulated, sounded as if it didn't get much practice. Since his home abutted the wetlands, he said, any development would have an impact on his view.

And on his seclusion, I thought.

He pointed to the Save the Bunker button on his lapel. "I'm also supporting the historical society in their efforts," he said. He went on to explain that the bunker, constructed during World War II to house a coastal artillery battery, was being considered for listing by the National Register of Historical Places. It would be demolished if development went forward.

"Though you may find the preservation of so recent and humble a site ludicrous, considering the ancient monuments of your own country, Mrs. Doolittle. But we southern Californians can't afford to squander what little history we have."

His crooked smile was strangely attractive, and I must confess I was quite charmed by his old-world formality. Despite his disfigurement, he had aged well and looked like a man in his sixties, though having served in World War II, he must have been seventy-odd.

We had been talking across Amelia, and when she engaged him in conversation, I turned my attention to the rest of the audience.

Near the exit on the upper level, Detective Mallory leaned against the wall, sipping from a plastic cup. He kept looking toward the door as if expecting someone. He caught me staring at him, and I looked away quickly.

I suspected that his presence here had more to do with the Jackson investigation than he had let on. Passions ran high over the fate of the wetlands. Caught in the middle of the controversy, it wasn't impossible that Bill had made enemies, any one of whom might have had a motive for killing him. I was relieved to think that Mallory wasn't totally focused on Rosemary as the prime suspect.

Across the auditorium, Dr. Willie chatted animatedly with Anthony "Tiptoe Tony" Tipton, an old surfing colleague of my late husband. Whether Tony came by his nickname from the way he scampered, surf-bound, across the hot sand, as some suggested, or from his occasional brushes with the law, as others less kindly disposed claimed, was open to question. But he was, in fact, a champion senior surfer, and I guessed that his concern for the coastline was the reason for his attending the meeting. His well-worn dark blue windbreaker, with Surfers Rule stencilled in four-inch white letters across the back, topped black O.P. surf shorts. A Surf City sport cap covered his sparse, downy pate.

He caught my eye, waved, and came over.

" 'Allo Mrs. D. Wot you doing 'ere, then?"

Then, seeing Mabel heading in our direction, he returned to his seat with an "Oh 'ell, I'll see you later." There was no love lost between those two.

But Mabel continued on down the aisle. She had larger game in view.

Sensing a good story, the media were there in force.

I recognized Lily Semple from our local *Surf City News*, and a photographer from the *Los Angeles Times*. Off to one side of the platform, a reporter from Channel 7 was interviewing a well-built, grey-haired woman who I recognized as the Commission chairperson from a picture in that morning's newspaper.

Mabel hovered behind them, trying to get her picket sign on camera.

Evie arrived, slipping into the seat next to mine, and sliding Chamois' tote bag under the seat. She showed not a hint that she'd arrived in a downpour. She wore an elegant St. John knit heather two-piece, with amethyst jewelry, her hair covered by a velvet beret in a deeper shade of purple, a soft tweed stole draped over her shoulders. A middle-aged Barbie in shrink-wrapped perfection.

The twelve commissioners, four women and eight men, filed in from an anteroom, and the chairperson brought the meeting to order. Her introductions were met with boos and catcalls from the rear of the auditorium.

Evie looked around in annoyance. "Who are these frightful people?" she said.

"Most of them are opposed to development," I said. "They think, rightly or wrongly, that the commissioners are in the developer's pocket."

Howard, who had exchanged his nautical outfit for a dark grey pin-striped suit, white shirt, and blue, grey, and white checked tie, looked mildly shell-shocked at the hostile reception. From a corner of the room where Mabel had button-holed the *Times* reporter, I saw her pointing in his direction. Making more mischief, no doubt.

The other more seasoned commissioners seemed to take the noisy reception in stride, one woman in a green hat going so far as to wave to the crowd, as if to adoring fans, before settling down and whispering behind her agenda to the tweedy, red-faced Colonel Blimp type on her right.

The chairperson opened the proceedings by asking a representative from the U.S. Army Corps of Engineers for an overview. Occasionally referring to a large map hanging on the wall behind the platform, he talked of flood control, retention basins, and underground water resources, all delivered in a dry, dispassionate manner. Whatever the outcome, he'd still have his job and his pension. I gave him a one on my zero-to-ten (ten being most likely to have murdered Bill Jackson) scale.

A studious-looking young man took the podium.

"That's John Palmer, from Bill Jackson's office," said Mabel who had taken a seat behind me. Reading from notes, it was obvious Palmer was ill-prepared to fill in for Bill at the last minute, limiting his remarks to an endorsement of a plan to create a tidal inlet that would connect the wetlands with the Pacific Ocean.

Only apparent motive: job advancement. I gave him a three.

Amelia leaned toward me and whispered, "He's a temporary replacement. Not nearly as well-informed as poor Bill was. Doesn't live in the area, for one thing. And I have heard . . ."

What Amelia had heard was lost in loud applause from the surfing contingent as Dr. Willie approached the podium.

"I'm here on behalf of the Southland Surfers," he said, charming the audience with his warm style. "We are opposed to the tidal inlet. It would cause beach and cliff erosion and would take away almost an acre of public beach.

"If you support our position, I urge you to attend our rally on the beach next Sunday. Let's all Take a Stand in the Sand."

Turning to see who was responsible for the loud whistles greeting this announcement (it was Tiptoe Tony), I was just in time to see Officer Offley enter through a side door and speak to Detective Mallory who, putting his coffee cup in a nearby trash bin, shrugged into his coat and made a hasty exit. I wondered if there had been a development in the Jackson case.

When the cheers subsided, an obviously smitten Green Hat asked Dr. Willie to repeat the date of the rally, making a note in a small diary she took from her purse. Colonel Blimp, under the mistaken impression that his mike was off, harrumped something about rabble rousers.

Not immune to Dr. Willie's charms myself, I had already dismissed him as a suspect. Like Amelia, he was too nice, too rational, to resort to violence to solve his problems.

Though most speakers favoured restoration and preservation of the wetlands, opinions differed widely as to exactly how this should be accomplished, and it was soon apparent that the proposed tidal inlet was the chief bone of contention.

Even among the pro-inlet forces, there were subfactions. Bird lovers, concerned about preservation of endangered species, wanted the nonnative red fox trapped and removed. Animal lovers argued that whether or not the red fox was indigenous was beside the point. He was here now. Trapping was cruel, relocation unworkable.

Many speakers felt that the only way to preserve the viability of the wetlands was to allow sea water to flow in, a natural process which had been halted some fifty years ago when oil had been discovered in the area. Others, however, including the surfing contingent, were more concerned about beach erosion and the depletion of available surfing area.

These differing agendas tended to work to the developer's advantage. The caveat "divide and conquer" could not have been better illustrated.

Why they couldn't work it out amongst themselves and present a united front against development was beyond me. That there needed to be some coalition among these various factions in order to defeat the proposed development seemed obvious to no one but myself.

Wildlife habitat was not all that was threatened by the bulldozer. Local Native Americans protested destruction of a sacred burial site, and the historical society made their plea for preservation of the bunker.

Evie moved restlessly. "I'm dying for a ciggie. How much longer, do you think?"

I had no idea. "You're watching democracy in action," I said. "It's tedious, but victory goes to those powerful enough or bloody-minded enough to stay the course."

Amelia's turn at the podium was listened to with quiet respect, her gentle voice drawing strength from her deep concern for the protected and endangered species that depended on the fragile marshland for survival.

"It is like the canary in the mine shaft," she warned. "What affects the ecology of the marsh, the food chain, will affect us all eventually."

Her moderation was in vivid contrast to Mabel's strident outburst a few minutes later.

Mabel had thrown in her lot with the pro-inlet group, as was apparent the minute she got up to speak. She finally had her audience, and she relished the moment.

Mindful of the threatening calls Howard had received, I listened carefully to what she had to say.

"There's people here, and I don't need no barge pole to touch 'em, that hope to grow rich from stealing our wetlands," she said, her gaze travelling slowly around the auditorium.

"Uh oh. Here it comes," I thought.

But Mabel's remarks were directed in a different quarter. Her eyes came to rest not on Howard but on a well-dressed business-type sitting in the front row.

"They'll stop at nothing to get what they want." Her voice shaking with emotion, she fixed him with an accusing glare. "Bill Jackson is lying dead not a mile from here, killed because he got in their way. Mark my words, they're not going to worry about killing animals!"

A shocked hush greeted Mabel's accusation.

Perhaps realizing that she had said too much, Mabel abruptly returned to her seat.

People fidgeted uncomfortably as the obvious target of her accusations took the podium and gave his name.

"Wesley Baines, vice president, Costa Bella Enterprises." Other than slightly flushed cheeks, he showed no sign that he realized Mabel's barbs were directed at him.

"Dishy," murmured Evie, taking a sudden interest in the proceedings. "Do we know him?"

I shook my head.

Tall, expensively dressed, fiftyish, he spoke of the benefits of an improved tax base and prosperity for the community.

"These people are misinformed. Development and restoration can both be achieved with our plan," said Baines, referring to his company's proposal to restore part of the deteriorating wetlands in exchange for permission to build on the remaining portion.

"Developer double-talk," Mabel hissed in my ear. "Destroy in order to save."

Millions of dollars were at stake here. Was it possible that Baines or his minions would resort to killing for profit? I gave him a seven on my likely-to-murder scale.

Describing the planned Spanish-style community, Baines continued. "Our vision is to make it seem like it was built a hundred years ago."

This was too much for Tony. "Then leave it alone, mate, if you want it to look like it was a hundred years ago," he cried.

"Order!" rapped the chairperson.

"Order?" shouted Tony. "I'll give you bloody order."

Evie touched my arm. "Isn't that the dear boy who saved Chamois' life?" she asked, referring to a previous escapade in pursuit of a stolen show dog.

"The dear boy who got us all into trouble in the first place, more like it," I replied.

Tony was making his way to the podium, removing his jacket to reveal a tee shirt bearing the same Surfers Rule legend. For all I knew, it was embroidered on his underwear, maybe even tattooed on his posterior.

"Mr. Baines, please continue," said the chairwoman.

But Baines, eyeing the advancing Tony in alarm,

apparently decided that discretion was the better part of valour and retreated to his seat.

Dr. Willie approached Tony, obviously intending to calm him down. But there was no stopping him. He had ridden Surf City's waves nearly every day for more than a quarter of a century. They were, perhaps, all that made his twilight years worthwhile. He had been waiting all evening to have his say, and he was not about to be shut up.

"There's been too much bloody development," he began. "So far, they haven't touched the waves. But now . . ." He shook his head sorrowfully, then continued.

"The way I see it, mates, is, well, it's a bloody carve-up, that's what it is. An inlet will wreck the waves. And what's Surf City without 'em? If this goes through, we may as well change the name to Concrete City, 'cos there ain't going to be no surf."

His wiry frame almost bouncing out of his sheepskin Ugg boots with indignation, he paused for breath, and was rewarded with a loud burst of applause.

Chamois, who had been growing increasingly restless as the evening wore on, now alarmed and frightened by all the agitation in the air, started yapping nervously.

The press photographers surged forward to get a closeup of Tony. Mabel, never one to miss a photo op, was on her feet.

"Habitat's more important than surfing, tha' great

lummox,'' she shouted, rushing at Tony, waving her sign.

"Stick to yer mangy cats, yer crazy old bird,'' Tony retorted.

"Are you putting it round that I'm barmy?'' she cried, coshing him on the head with the sign.

• 7 •
The Morning After

UNABLE TO RESTORE order, the chair had eventually been obliged to adjourn the meeting. No arrests had been made, no thanks to Tony and Mabel, who had done their best to get a punch-up going.

I had hurried home to the peace and quiet of my cottage, resolving to Watson that I washed my hands of the lot of them.

Evie and Howard had fled back to the sanctuary of their club. They were headed north to Santa Barbara the following day for the next public hearing. I hoped for their sakes that the agenda there proved to be less contentious than the one in Surf City.

They planned to be back in the area for the third meeting, to be held in Long Beach.

Evie's parting words had dealt with a subject far more crucial. "Do try to do something with your hair before I get back," she said. "We'll both feel so much better."

I slept late the next morning, and was, in fact, still on my first cup of tea, when the telephone broke in on my not entirely charitable reflections of that remark.

"Delilah Doolittle, pet detective," I answered, hoping a new assignment was coming my way.

"Delilah. It's Mabel. What did you think of the meeting?"

"I hardly know what to think. Not much was accomplished, other than to let everybody have their say. And how much influence that will have in stopping the development is anyone's guess. Certainly you all gave the commissioners something to mull over."

"Those commissioners!" she declared. "I wouldn't give a cup of cold water for the lot of 'em. All in Costa Bella's pocket, you mark my words."

"But they have to consider public opinion, surely," I replied, "and even their own staff seems to be in favour of preserving the wetlands."

"Well, we'll see about that when it comes to a vote. But you're very naive, Delilah, if you think that money and influence aren't going to be very important here. That's why we must do something to stop them."

I didn't like the "we", and I wasn't really interested in Mabel's schemes, but keeping in mind the threatening calls Howard had received, I let her talk.

"Like what?" I asked.

"Well, I've been doing some snooping around, and I've come up with something very interesting."

"Really?"

"Now, where did I put it?" There was the sound of rustling paper, then: "I know I left it right here on the table last night, all ready for when I called you this morning. Let me think a minute. Mack and Zelda got in a fight, and I had to go and separate them. A carton of milk got knocked over, and I had to clean that up. Oh, now I remember. While I was doing that, one of the cats peed on the paper, and I put it outside to dry off. Any road up, I'd like your opinion."

This chain of events left me nonplussed, but I soldiered on. "What did you have in mind?"

"Can we meet for a coffee sometime today? At the diner in the park?"

At any other time I would have begged off, social chitchat with Mabel not being my idea of a good time. But out of concern for Howard, I reluctantly decided it was as well to humour her.

"I'm busy all morning," I said. "How about lunchtime, around one o'clock?"

"All right. See you then. 'Bye."

I showered and dressed: jeans and a green cable-knit sweater I'd bought on my last trip home to England; thick socks. Though the rain had eased up, it was still chilly. Then I turned my attention to work, checking the lost and found ads, mailing flyers about the lost Puli to all the shelters in the area, and doing some billing, though this last task took grievously little time. Business was slow.

Belatedly, I rang Dr. Willie. In all the uproar over

the murder and then Evie's arrival, I had almost forgotten poor Hobo.

"Delilah," he said. "I was just going to call you to report on the cat. I'm afraid we can't save the leg. Too much nerve damage. But he should make a good recovery. You can pick him up in a day or so. He may as well recuperate with you as stay in a hospital cage here. Did you find out any more about the traps?"

"No, I didn't pursue it. Bill Jackson's death put it right out of my mind. I'll call his deputy as soon as I hang up. John Palmer, I believe his name is. Do you know him?"

"Never met him before last night." He paused, then said, "What did you think of the meeting?"

"What in the world got into Tony?" I asked. "He seems to be taking this threat to his waves as a personal affront."

"He's going to get himself into serious trouble if he keeps that up," agreed the vet. "I mean, we're all concerned, but with Tony it's getting to be an obsession."

Next I put in a call to John Palmer at Parks and Rec. He wasn't there, but a secretary assured me that there was no recent record of any trap permits having been issued.

"He was a real softie over the animals," she said. I could hear the tears in her voice. "He would have been very reluctant to issue any permit for trapping, and I'm certain he wouldn't have given a verbal okay.''

It was mid-morning, time for ''elevenses'', and I was just about to put the kettle on when I heard a car pull up in the driveway. Watson was on her feet, alerting me to a stranger.

I opened the door to find Detective Mallory about to ring the bell.

''Do you always open your door without checking who's there?'' chided the policeman.

I pointed to Watson, standing firm, ears erect, ready to do battle.

''No one crosses my threshold without Watson's approval,'' I said. She did indeed look intimidating. In reality, she was a pussycat, but no stranger seeing her in her attack stance would take a chance on putting her to the test.

''Come in. To what do I owe the pleasure?'' I was indeed curious as to the purpose of his visit. I didn't think there was anything I could add to the statement I'd made after discovering Bill Jackson's body.

''I was just going to make a pot of tea,'' I said. ''Would you like a cup? Or perhaps you'd prefer a coffee?''

''Tea will be fine. It's a long time since I've had a cup of real English tea,'' he said, following me into the kitchen.

''I believe you said your family was from England,'' I said.

''Yes, from Taunton, in Devon. Do you know it?''

"Lovely part of the country," I offered.

I plugged in the electric kettle and set out my Wedgewood tea service, usually reserved for special occasions. I wondered if I should offer him something to eat. But what? Unaccountably, I found myself wishing I had made some of my special shortbread biscuits. Though why in the world this thought should occur, I could not for the life of me fathom. I hadn't made shortbread or much of anything else since Roger died.

"Do you take milk in your tea?" I asked. "Or is that too English for you?"

"Milk's fine."

He was improving by the minute.

I handed him a cup and saucer, and he sat down. Watson put her head in his lap.

"She seems to like me," he said, patting her head.

"You're sitting in her chair," I answered, embarrassed that his nice dark grey slacks were about to be covered in red dog hair.

He stood up suddenly. "My apologies," he said to Watson, who immediately took his place.

"Let's go in the sitting-room, it's more comfortable," I said. Then, in a shameless attempt to learn more about his personal life, I asked, "Do you have pets?" I hoped this might give me an insight into his domestic arrangements.

"No. I'm not home enough to give a pet the attention it needs."

Aha. Then there was probably no Mrs. Mallory or

significant other to share pet-owning duties.

"Now, how can I help you?" I asked, when he was settled, this time in one of my more respectable armchairs.

"We're having trouble locating Jackson's wife," he said. "No one seems to have any idea where she is. All we have is Mrs. Redpath's statement that she saw her leave in a taxi."

He helped himself to sugar from the bowl on the tea tray, stirred his tea, and continued. "We traced the taxi and found out that it took her to LAX, International Departures. We interviewed the cab driver last night."

That probably accounted for his abrupt departure from the meeting.

"She caught the 8:45 a.m. Delta flight to Paris," he went on, "but from there we've lost track of her. As far as we can tell, she didn't make any advance hotel reservations. We have Interpol looking for her, but we haven't been able to give them much to go on."

"Now, hang on a minute," I said, nettled. "You surely don't seriously suspect Rosemary of murdering her husband. Why, they were the happiest of couples, been married for twenty years or more."

"You have to admit, it does look suspicious," he said.

"I don't have to admit any such thing."

He took a sip of tea. "It's odd that she's left no trace of where she was going," he went on. "You'd think she'd leave her husband an itinerary. Quite apart from that, of course, we need to inform her of his death as soon as possible.''

I was duly admonished.

''You're a friend of theirs,'' he said. ''Can you give me any idea of family members we might contact?''

''As far as I know, there was just the two of them. No children. They'd always regretted that.'' I thought for a minute, then added, ''I do recall Rosemary mentioning a sister. Apparently she disappeared many years ago. They'd never been able to trace her. Very sad. But that's all I know.'' I sighed. ''Rosemary's going to be devastated when she gets back.''

''If she gets back,'' said Mallory. ''Right now she's our prime suspect.''

''Well, you're dead wrong, Detective Mallory.'' I was really angry now. ''In all the years I've known Bill and Rosemary, I never heard a cross word exchanged between them. How do you know Rosemary isn't lying dead somewhere?''

''Mrs. Redpath saw her get into a taxi, and the taxi delivered her to LAX,'' he reminded me patiently.

So much for my powers of deduction.

There was little point in pursuing the argument. Neither one of us knew exactly what had happened in the Jacksons' kitchen.

In an apparent effort to change the subject, Mallory looked around the sitting room. Nothing would escape that keen gaze, and I was acutely aware that it was some considerable time since I'd cleaned house. His eyes rested on one of my bird photographs.

"That's very good," he said, taking a closer look. "Did you take it?"

"Yes. Out on the wetlands, by the bridge. A lucky grab shot," I answered, somewhat ungraciously.

He asked if I was planning to attend an upcoming wildlife art exhibit, to be presented by the local chapter of the Audubon Society. I said I had been thinking about it. He hesitated for a moment, and I thought he might have been about to invite me to go with him. I was trying to decide what my answer would be when a rap at the back door put an end to all such speculation.

" 'Allo. Anybody 'ome?" It was Tiptoe Tony, with less than perfect timing.

"Tony," I said. "This is a surprise."

Mallory got to his feet as Tony entered the sitting room with Trixie, his Jack Russell terrier, at his heels.

Watson and Trixie sniffed noses in recognition, while Mallory and Tony exchanged the briefest of greetings and eyed each other suspiciously. Their acquaintance was of a professional nature, on opposite sides of the law. Tony, though he had declared many times that he had retired, had a reputation as a petty thief and had had more than one run-in with Detective Mallory.

Tony lifted the teapot lid, saw that there was some tea left and, without invitation, poured himself a cup.

Mallory, taking in Tony's familiarity with my teapot with what I feared was entirely the wrong impression, prepared to leave.

"Well, if you think of anything, I'd appreciate it if you'd let me know," he said stiffly as I saw him out.

"What's 'e doing 'ere?" asked Tony, before Mallory was decently out of earshot.

· 8 ·

Doggie House-Guest

"I MIGHT WELL ask you the same thing, Tony," I said. "After your performance last night . . ."

"I told them a thing or three, didn't I?" he interrupted, a grin wrinkling his tanned, lined face.

Really, Tony's behaviour seemed to worsen with age. Growing old disgracefully, one might say. There was a cockiness about him that advancing years failed to diminish.

His only concession to the chill weather: He had exchanged his customary OP surf shorts for a pair of faded, tattered jeans. Tanned toes clung to blue rubber thongs.

"You didn't do your cause much good, carrying on like that," I said.

"Well," he said, somewhat chastened. "These inlanders come to town, chuck their money around, and think they can walk all over us."

"That may well be. But I really don't have time to hear it all again, Tony. I'm sorry to rush you, but I have to go out soon."

I thought it best not to tell him I was meeting Mabel. I didn't want to set him off again.

"What's on your mind?" I asked. "Other than that, I mean?"

"I was wondering if you could look after Trixie for a couple of days. The storm's brought some great waves, and some of the lads want to go down to Trestles overnight," he said, referring to one of California's best surfing areas, a rocky-bottomed point break south of San Clemente. "Thought I'd better go along to keep an eye on them."

The idea of Tiptoe Tony being a stabilizing influence on anyone was cause for amusement, but I refrained from comment.

It was not the first time I had been called upon to take care of Trixie, though in the past the request had been more along the lines of "I'm in the clink, can you take care of me dog?"

I looked at Watson. She was eyeing Trixie with dismay as the little terrier sniffed at her food bowl. Too well bred to snap, Watson cast a pleading look in my direction.

"What do you think, Watson," I said. "Would you like Trixie to stay?"

Her response was to go under the kitchen table (her hideaway when trouble was brewing), put her chin on her paws, and glare at the intruder.

I turned back to Tony. "You heard about Bill Jackson, of course?"

"Yes," he said, interest and concern showing on

his face. "I 'ear you was the one that found 'im."

I nodded. "It was a shock, I can tell you. And no sign of Rosemary. In fact that's why Mallory was here. He wondered if I might know where she could be."

"She was going over the pond, wasn't she, sometime soon?"

"Apparently so. But the police lost track of her after Paris. How did you know?"

"I ran into her a week or so ago. She said something about she'd got some real important news from friends over there and was planning a trip. Was real excited."

He checked to see if there was any more tea in the pot, squeezed out half a cup, then said, "Mallory don't think she had something to do with it, does 'e?"

"From what he said this morning, I rather think that he does."

"That's bloody daft." Tony frowned. "Even money that Costa Bella crowd are at the bottom of it."

"I'm not so sure of that either," I said. "They may be ruthless. There's a lot of money at stake. But surely they would stop short of violence. I'm wondering if it has something to do with whoever's setting the traps."

Tony shook his head sadly as I told him about Hobo, recovering at Dr. Willie's.

"Poor little sod," he said. "Out by the bunker, you say. Bloody eyesore, that is. Something about that place gives me the creeps. Wouldn't bovver me none if they got rid of it. Historical landmark my arse," he snorted. "They'll be putting plaques on 7-Elevens next."

Trixie pawed at his leg, and he rubbed her ear idly as he continued, "I remember years ago, before your time, there was something or other going on there. People said they'd seen lights out there at night. Police investigated but never found nothing. Said it was just kids. But I often wondered about it."

He eyed me critically. "What you done to yer 'air?"

My hands flew to my head. "Whatever do you mean?"

"Dunno. It looks different."

"Don't you start. I get enough of that from Evie."

"Oh. Mrs. Cavendish. Wonderful woman. How's she doing? I saw her at the 'earing last night. 'Er old man's on the Coastal Commission now, right?"

I nodded.

" 'Ere, maybe I can talk to him about the bloody inlet. What's his phone number?"

"Really, Tony, I would prefer you didn't use my friends to . . ."

"Hey, I'm a citizen, ain't I?" he interrupted. "What you think I went through all that immigration palaver for? Got to exercise me rights."

"Well, exercise them down at City Hall, or write a letter, then," I said tartly. I prided myself on not exploiting my friends to my advantage, and I wasn't going to allow Tony to do so.

Pointedly, I looked at my watch. Tony took the hint and, wiping his mouth with the back of his hand, stood up, getting ready to leave.

"Thanks for the tea, luv. Here's Trixie's suitcase." He indicated a large plastic shopping bag he had brought in with him. From experience, I knew it contained her bed, leash, food dish, a couple of tins of dog food, and her tennis ball.

"I'll slip out quick-like before she notices," he said, nodding at Trixie, now nose deep in Watson's kibble.

He tiptoed out, closing the kitchen door quietly behind him.

I rinsed the tea-cups, clipped Trixie's leash to her collar, and with Watson at my heels, headed out the door.

Mabel awaited.

• 9 •
Bone Appetite

"WHAT'S IT GOING to be, ladies?" I asked my canine companions as we settled down for lunch at the outdoor Doggie Diner.

I had decided to get there early before Mabel arrived. We would enjoy lunch by the duck pond, then the dogs could run loose for a while in the nearby bark park. It had stopped raining for the nonce, but I could tell from the cool breeze and the dark clouds that more rain was on the way. I was glad I had worn my sweater.

Watson sniffed the Canine Cuisine menu appreciatively, her nose passing over the Hot Diggity hot-dog and the Hound Dog Heaven hamburger patty, coming to rest at the Wrangler Roundup ground turkey patty "for those on low-cal diets."

"Good choice, girl," I said, approvingly. "A lady should always watch her waistline. How about you, Trixie?"

But Trixie, straining at the leash, was more interested in the tenants of the nearby pond. Duck was her preference.

"Trixie will have the same," I said to Jennie the waitress who, with pencil and pad in one hand petted Watson with the other.

From the people menu I selected the veggie sandwich and a glass of lemonade.

"I'm meeting Mabel Redpath here later," I told Jennie when she returned with our order.

Jennie, who knew most of her customers by name—the pets, if not their owners—clicked her tongue in dismay.

"Oh, shoot, is she coming?" she said, stooping to set down water for the dogs. "She's practically not allowed here anymore, you know. The boss says the next time she bothers the other customers about getting their pets fixed, he's going to ask her to leave."

The scent of the turkey patty finally got Trixie's attention, and before I could stop her she had jumped up onto the seat next to mine, then onto the table, her claws skittering for traction on the plastic, and knocking over my lemonade in the process.

Patiently, as one well experienced with this kind of behaviour, Jennie pointed to the sign indicating that canine customers were not allowed on the furniture.

I forked the turkey patties into pieces, and placed two paper plates on the ground. Lunch was quickly disposed of, and Trixie once again turned her attention to the ducks, straining at her leash which I had looped around a leg of my chair.

The outdoor café was a popular hang-out for pet owners, especially on the weekends when the place was full to capacity with dog-walkers, dog-joggers and dog-skateboarders. But today we practically had the place to ourselves, except for an elderly couple who had circumvented the Please Keep Dogs off the Furniture sign by taking turns holding their overweight pug on their laps. The dog was too heavy to hold for very long, and when it started to slide off the lap of one, the other would take over.

A short distance away, under the willow trees, a fisherman cast his line over the water. I hoped there were no ducks within his range.

I finished my sandwich and checked my watch. Mabel would be here soon. There was just enough time for Watson and Trixie to have a run before she arrived.

"Come along, girls. Time to go," I said, picking up the leashes. Watson was on her feet immediately. But Trixie's leash dangled loosely by my chair. Her leather collar, worn through with age where the clasp had rubbed it, lay empty at my feet.

She wasn't hard to find. Turning my head in the direction of her yapping, I saw she had put the ducks to flight, the mallards skimming across the surface of the water, just out of doggie reach, quacking in panic.

Not for nothing was Trixie a surfer's dog. I had watched her attempt to paddle out to Tony's board on many occasions. Tossed back on the beach by the surf, she would roll over, shake, and with terrier tenacity, paddle out again and again. Now, with no surf to slow her down, she paddled determinedly after the mallards, blissfully ignorant of the Please Do Not Harass the Ducks sign.

I watched helplessly. With her boundless energy, Trixie could keep this up for hours. The water wasn't very deep. Was there any point in my wading in after her? Probably not. The pond was large, accommodating several small islands, on any one of which she could land, catch her breath, and be off again before I could reach her.

I silently cursed Tony for not replacing her collar. My futile "Trixie, heel! Trixie, come!" and "Trixie, you bad girl!" were lost in a chorus of yapping and quacking.

Watson stood beside me, wagging her stumpy tail and uttering an occasional bark. Though she knew better than to join Trixie in her escapade, I suspected she was enjoying the fact that the little terrier was in trouble.

So intent was I on keeping Trixie in view, I didn't notice that the fisherman had abandoned his rod and line and was wading across to the island where the ducks were headed. He was now closing in on the terrier, who was about to clamber up the bank to give chase on land. With a quick toss of his landing net, the fisherman scooped up a wriggling, yelping, and very startled little dog.

Firmly closing the mouth of the net, the man waded back across the narrowest part of the pond to deposit the wet and muddy truant in my arms. A duck feather hung from her mouth, another peeped out from behind her ear. Keeping a tight hold on the scruff of her neck, for the first time I took a good look at the rescuer.

To my surprise, it was Bud Hefner, the World War II vet I'd met at last night's meeting.

"Thank you so much," I stammered, embarrassed by Trixie's disgraceful behaviour and discomfited by what was, to all appearances, my lack of control of my dog.

In the harsh daylight, Hefner's scarred face took on an almost sinister cast, and I could easily understand the reason for his solitary existence. I was all the more appreciative of his assistance.

He waved aside my thanks. "She was scaring the fish," he said brusquely.

I wasn't to be put off so easily. I was intrigued by this mystery man, and wanted to get to know him better.

"At least let me buy you a cup of coffee," I said, quite forgetting my appointment with Mabel. "Warm you up after your unexpected plunge."

"No need for that." He placed a hand against a nearby tree and surveyed a wading boot, lifting it for my confirmation. "You see, the water didn't even reach the top."

"No. I insist. Just give me a minute to shut this little nuisance in the car," I said, indicating my station wagon parked nearby.

Several more cars had arrived while we were eating lunch, and in order to reach the rear door of the wagon I had to squeeze past a black Volkswagen Beetle that had parked too close, snagging my sweater on an oversized sideview mirror as I did so. With a gasp of annoyance, I hastily deposited Trixie in the back of my car, and grabbed a towel for Hefner from the odd assortment I carried for doggy emergencies.

''Now, about that coffee,'' I said, as he finished drying his hands and arms.

I turned as I heard a ''Yoo-hoo'' from the just-arriving Mabel.

When I turned back again, Hefner was gone.

· 10 ·

The Muttley Crew

"ONE AT A time now; I don't have arms in the back of my head, you know," Mabel admonished her charges, vainly attempting to control the flock of unruly cockerpoos that tumbled out of her car, all barking excitedly.

It was obvious that Mabel had a preference for cockerpoos. The medium-sized cross-breeds looked as if they might all be distantly related to each other. Each had a modicum of poodle or cocker spaniel (or both) in its lineage, with shaggy or curly coats in assorted colours: grey, white, black, beige, brown.

"Was that Bud Hefner?" she asked, sorting out the leashes of half a dozen dogs. "You are honored. He's sly, that one. Barely ever ventures out, much less talks to anyone. Just as well, I suppose, with that face. Fortunately, I usually only see him at night, when I'm feeding the ferals."

The thought that her opinion of Hefner probably had more to do with his unfortunate appearance than anything else did nothing to endear her to me. In any event, if she was hoping for some juicy gossip, she was doomed to disappointment.

"Shall we walk a bit first, before we have coffee?" she continued. "The dogs have been cooped up all morning. Ee by gum, I'm that busy. Had to go to the discount grocery outlet on my way here. They give me expired cottage cheese and milk. I tell 'em it's for the pets, but there's nothing wrong with it. I eat it myself." She put two fingers to her mouth and did a sly grin. "Why run up a big bill on my revolting charge account when I can eat for free?"

Why indeed?

I checked that Trixie was locked securely in the station wagon. The weather was cool; with the windows cracked, and parked under a tree, she would be comfortable enough. Then, bringing Watson to heel, we set off on the path that encircled the duck pond, eventually bringing us back to the diner.

Our progress was hampered by Mabel's dogs continually tugging her in several different directions.

"Now Brownie, stop that," she would say, or "Zelda, you mustn't," as the undisciplined Brownie, Zelda, and company did exactly as they pleased, limited only by the length of their leashes, and often nearly tripping Mabel in the process.

Poor Watson had her work cut out trying to stay out of their way. As did I.

Mabel's outfit was very similar to the one she'd been wearing at Bill Jackson's house the other morning, no doubt plucked from a whole wardrobe full of mismatched sweat tops and bottoms. I suspected she might be colour-blind, and that at home there was a green top and a pink bottom to match the pink top and green bottom she was wearing today. She was wearing the same red knit cap. Her worn tennis shoes were tied with odd-coloured laces, the soles duct-taped to the uppers.

Her appearance belied her circumstances. She was comfortably off, though this had not always been the case. Until her husband had died a few years previously, she'd had to work two part-time jobs in order to finance her animal rescue activities.

Now that she had her house to herself and the proceeds of a nice life insurance policy to sustain her, Mabel was dangerously close to becoming a collector—one of those people who are unable to control the urge to take in every stray animal that comes their way, eventually ending up the subject of grim newspaper stories when animal control and the health department have to be called in.

In between untangling herself from an assortment of leashes, which ran the gamut from rolled English leather to nylon, rope, and bits of string, Mabel kept up a running commentary on the dogs' histories.

"What do you think of my muttley crew?" she asked, with what I was sure was an entirely unintentional play on words.

Without waiting for my reply, for which, in any case, I was at a total loss, she continued. "Zelda," she indicated a small honey-coloured dog with a bushy tail, "I got out of the 'free to you' column in the *Surf City News*. I check every week to see what people are giving away. Her owner gave her up because he was moving. Me, I'd live in a tent before I gave up one of my animals."

"That's Fabian," she said of an older stiff-legged grey dog who had brought us all to a halt while he stopped to sniff at a trash can. "He was tied to a tree over by the library. You know, the big oak by the parking lot. He looked that poorly. All skin and bones. I waited for a while to see if the owner was coming back, then I took him home."

"How about that one?" I asked indicating a sad-looking black dog wearing a bright red knitted jacket with white snowflake design, which it obviously hated. Every few minutes, the unfortunate creature would stop for a scratch, and bite at the jacket as if trying to get rid of it.

"Oh, the poor thing. You wouldn't believe the state she was in. I had to shave her down practically to the skin, she was that matted. That's why I put the sweater on her. Didn't want her to catch cold, especially since she's just been spayed."

"Where did she come from?"

"I found her wandering in the street."

"Did you call the shelter? The owner might be looking for her."

Mabel sniffed. "Letting her get in that state, they don't deserve to get her back. I'll find her a good home."

Mabel always professed that her charges were in her care only temporarily. But her standards were so impossibly high that few people qualified for one of her orphans. It's been said that it was easier to adopt a child than one of Mabel's strays.

The path wound back toward the diner, and I was beginning to wonder if she had forgotten the purpose of our meeting.

"What was it you wanted to speak to me about?" I asked, a little impatiently.

"What? Oh, yes. It's about poor Bill Jackson. You know, I told the police everything . . ." She paused. "Well, not exactly everything. I told them that I saw Rosemary leave in a taxi that morning. I answered all their questions, but when I tried to tell them my suspicions, they weren't interested. Got quite rude, in fact."

"Really? What suspicions?"

Mabel turned around on the pathway, untwisting herself from a veritable Maypole of leashes.

"Well, I think the Costa Bella crowd have something to do with it."

She wasn't the only one. Amelia the previous evening, and Tony that morning had expressed similar opinions.

"Do you have anything to go on?"

"Aye. I think Bill had evidence that would prove that the land is in the public domain. Once that got out, it would mean an end to development. Nip it in the butt once and for all."

Poor Wesley Baines, first threatened by Tony, now in danger of being nipped in the butt by Mabel.

"And," she lowered her voice. "Like I told the police, that Rosemary Jackson, coming and going at all hours of the night. Who knows what she was up to. I wouldn't put it past her . . ."

"Of course she's out at night. She works the night shift at the hospital," I broke in hastily.

"Well, that's as may be," said Mabel, reluctant to let go of her theory. "But maybe she was seeing somebody on the sly. Maybe it was that Wesley Baines." She leaned toward me, her eyes narrowing, and her voice even lower. "Maybe she was helping him get the land—and that's why Bill got killed. Killing two birds with one stone," she finished triumphantly.

And maybe Mabel was letting her imagination run away with her. Now she was hinting at a conspiracy between Rosemary and the developers.

"But you have to have proof," I said weakly, unsure which of these flying accusations to tackle first.

"Happen I do," she replied triumphantly.

"You do?" I was surprised.

"Well," she hedged. "I don't exactly have it all together yet, just bits and pieces. That's where you come in. Would you do some checking? You're so clever, Delilah. So much better at that sort of thing than I am. After all, you *are* a detective. We're willing to pay you."

That made it more interesting. "We?"

"SSCOWL. It would be considered part of our overall effort."

We had by then arrived back at the Doggie Diner. Having already eaten lunch, I just ordered coffee. I never drink tea out. I have yet to find a decent cup of tea outside of my own kitchen.

"I'll have a bran muffin with mine," said Mabel. Then to me, "Give mesself a treat. This is a special occasion, Delilah. You and me working together."

I groaned inwardly.

I waited until Jennie brought our order, then said, "Really, Mabel, I don't know."

It was more than my dislike of Mabel that made me hesitate. There was so much discord over the wetlands, even my friends were at odds. And to be working even on the fringe of a police investigation and to risk running afoul of Detective Mallory once again seemed unwise. My instincts told me this was something I should observe from the sidelines.

Further, I mused, watching the muttley crew weave an intricate lattice of leashes around table and chair legs, sniffing for crumbs, despite her eccentricities, Mabel was nobody's fool. I only half believed she knew anything at all. She might well be using me for a fishing expedition. Or maybe she expected me to turn up something incriminating about Howard, choosing this as a way of bringing it to my attention.

Concern for Evie and Howard was uppermost in my mind. I didn't want to offend Mabel by coming right out and asking her if she had made the telephone threats. If she was the culprit, she certainly wouldn't tell me. And if she didn't know anything about them, I would have given her more grist for her gossip mill.

Spreading her muffin with butter, Mabel accidentally dropped a few crumbs on the floor. A dog squabble ensued. Having calmed them down, giving a crumb of muffin to each and every one, Mabel continued to press her case.

"It would only take a few hours of your time, Delilah. One day at most. I'm such a dunce, I wouldn't know where to start."

The way she pronounced "such" and "dunce", in the shaped vowels of her native Yorkshire, triggered nostalgia for home, and I found myself nodding in agreement.

"All right," I said. "I'll do some checking for you. But just as a favour. I don't want to be officially involved."

"That's champion. Thanks, lass."

"Where's this evidence you spoke of?" I asked.

"I put it in me bum bag for safety," she said, fumbling in her fanny pack. "Oops, no I didn't. I remember. I meant to, and then one of the dogs . . . Oh, never mind. I'll bring it by later."

This was the second time she had managed to avoid giving me any direct proof, strengthening my suspicion that maybe she was having me on.

Business taken care of, Mabel turned her attention to the passing parade of dog walkers.

"You should get her spayed, you know," she

called to a young couple walking by with a Boxer in an advanced state of pregnancy. "Too many unwanted dogs in the world now!"

The dog might have been a champion breeding bitch for all she knew. But that wouldn't cut any ice with Mabel.

The couple hurried on, with an occasional backward glance at the strange woman in the red hat.

Behind Mabel's back, Jennie rolled her eyes expressively.

As for me, I was already regretting my decision to aid in SSCOWL's investigation.

. 11 .

Eye Opener

"ECO-WARRIORS STRIKE BLOW for Coastal Protection."

The front-page headline leaped out at me as I picked up the *Los Angeles Times* from the driveway.

I almost dropped the paper in dismay on closer examination of the large colour photograph that accompanied the article. Prominent among the figures waving signs "Surfers Rule" was none other than Tiptoe Tony himself, chained to a bulldozer.

I walked back into the house, reading about the arrest the previous day of the protesters who had attempted to halt exploratory work at the head of the proposed wetlands inlet.

I looked down at Trixie who, along with Watson, had followed me out to the driveway.

"Your dad's really been and gone and done it this time, Trix," I said to her, in language her master might have used. "Listen to this."

The little terrier cocked her head to one side in apparent interest as I read aloud.

"Protesters arrived at the site before dawn and, in a symbolic gesture, one of them secured himself to a bulldozer with a bicycle lock.

"Once freed from the bulldozer, the demonstrator was given the chance to leave without being arrested for trespassing, but he refused, saying he'd just as soon go to jail and make a statement.

" 'We are not giving up without a fight. This is a pre-emptive strike. It's the only way to get their attention,' he stated.

"When asked his name, the demonstrator replied, 'John Bloody Bull.' "

"That's your dad talking," I said to Trixie, whose only response was to look at me, her dark brown eyes pleading forgiveness for her master's transgressions.

I'm rather afraid that Watson looked a little smug.

I re-heated the kettle and mashed the tea. This called for a third cup.

So this was why Tony had enlisted my assistance. Surfing at Trestles, was he? Keeping an eye on the lads, was he? Some of the "lads" looked nearly as old as he was.

I was shocked by his tactics, and any sympathy I might have had for him and his cause was lost in the rush of annoyance I felt that he had lied to me.

I read the rest of the paper in silence, dawdling over my tea, then contemplated my day.

Dark clouds gathering over the ocean told me that rain was definitely in the offing. It was a good day to stay home. But I had things to do.

I had spent most of the previous day in a fruitless search for Mariah the Puli, checking shelters from Long Beach to Oceanside. Though I had issued a general BOLO (be on the look out for) I could not be sure that kennel attendants would recognize a Puli if one did show up. It was safer to look in person. This time I had asked them to check their DOA lists. Nothing resembling a Puli, or its relative the larger Komondor, had been reported.

Well, she hadn't just vanished into thin air. She was out there somewhere, and I was determined to find her.

This morning I planned to stop by Dr. Willie's to pick up Hobo. Later, I would turn my attention to Mabel's assignment. I hadn't done anything about it yesterday, and she'd be calling me soon for a progress report.

But Trixie underfoot provided a constant reminder of Tony's escapade, and it was no surprise when he called me a little while later.

"'Allo, Mrs. D. It's me, Tony."

"I know who it is. What in the world do you think you're doing?"

"You 'eard about the caper, then?"

"It would be hard not to, since it's all over the front page of the *Times* this morning."

"Get away," he crowed, clearly delighted. "That's brilliant. We'll show 'em."

"Not so much of the 'we'. You can leave me out of it, and you can start by picking up Trixie. I have to collect that cat today, and I'm not sure they'll get along.''

''Well, that's a bit tricky at the moment, luv,'' he said. ''I'm still in the nick.''

Here it comes, I thought. But I'm not going to offer. He's going to have to ask me. I waited.

''Could you come and pick me up, luv?'' he said. ''Me car's still out at the site.''

''It'll have to be later on. I'm busy most of the day.''

Tony could jolly well cool his heels. Right now I had to see a man about a cat.

· 12 ·
Storm Warning

I MANAGED TO find a parking spot in the narrow, one-way streets that served the beachside community. I wouldn't have been so lucky during the summer, but now, mid-week and off-season, and the weather bad, there was little beach traffic. Still, I wondered, not for the first time, why Dr. Willie didn't have his office in a place more accessible to his clients. But, if truth be told, he cared little for his small-animal practice, much preferring to spend his time in rescue and re-habilitation of the local wildlife, primarily shorebirds and raptors, the invariable losers in any confrontation with man, his automobiles, his fishhooks, and his pel-let guns.

There was no answer to my knock on the front door. Guessing that Dr. Willie would be on the beach, I walked down the narrow side passage to check.

He was just coming out of the surf, his wet suit dripping; his long, straight black hair escaped from the usual neat ponytail, whipped around his face in the wind. In one hand he held a pair of fins, in the other a surf leash, at the end of which waddled a California brown pelican.

He waved as he unlatched the gate in the low, wooden fence that separated the house from the beach.

"Come on in, Delilah," said the vet. "Let me get Percy settled, and I'll be right with you."

He led the bird to an outdoor enclosure equipped with low perches and a small wading pool, explaining that its wing had been badly damaged by a pellet gun, and it would never be able to fly well enough to be released back into the wild.

As if on cue, Percy, now perched on a piece of driftwood, his feathers slick from his dip in the ocean, stretched out his wings to dry, the left one hanging awkwardly, the wrist shattered beyond repair.

I stepped nearer for a better look.

"Don't get too close," Dr. Willie warned. "That bill is razor sharp.

"I take him with me when I go body surfing, if there're not too many people around," he continued. "Gives him some exercise, and keeps him in touch with the waves."

The sun, momentarily breaking through the lowering dark clouds, glinted off the bird's eyes, which gleamed like plastic buttons on either side of its narrow, bony head. They seemed to follow a squadron of his brethren, just then passing low over the waves in a powerful stroking flight. The missing man formation?

Snap out of it Delilah, I told myself. You're getting sentimental in your old age. But the thought persisted. Did Percy yearn to join them? Were his instincts at this moment impelling him to try?

Dr. Willie followed my gaze, then reached into a nearby tank, extracted a wriggling herring, and tossed it to the bird, who caught it expertly in its sculpted beak.

We entered the house by a side door, passing an examining room and the surgery, on to the hospital area, where several patients, including a burrowing owl and an iguana, as well as the usual dogs and cats, were in various stages of recovery.

"If you'll wait here for a minute, I'm going to go change," said the vet.

He returned wearing grey sweats, his wet hair once again tied back off his face. Sand still clung to his bare feet.

Reaching into one of the cages, he removed Hobo to an examining table, checked his dressing, and said, "He's still a little groggy from the medication, but he'll be fine. I'll give you some antibiotics for him. The sutures can come out in a couple of weeks."

Placing the patient in the plastic carrier I had brought with me, he said, "Did you see Tony's picture in the *Times* this morning?"

"I most certainly did." I said. "His behaviour at the hearing the other night was bad enough, and now this . . ."

"He wanted me to go with him."

"Then you knew! Why didn't you stop him?"

"I tried. The night of the hearing." He shook his head. "He was real mad at me because I told him to forget it."

I remembered wondering what they could be talking about so heatedly.

"Why didn't you go?"

"I'm too busy here, for one thing." He gestured around the room, taking in his patients. "Besides, I'm like you, Delilah. Always hoping sweet reason will win in the end."

He smiled, then continued. "I thought Tony was going to deck Mabel the other evening. But she can be a pain."

No argument there. I nodded in agreement as he went on. "She's always in here with one or another of her flock. I've tried to persuade her to keep the numbers down, but every time she comes in, she's got a new orphan with her. Not to mention the feral cats she brings in for spaying or neutering."

"That must cost a packet," I said, mindful of the bill I was running up for Hobo's treatment.

"I don't think money's a problem for Mabel," he replied. "But it's a lot of work for her to take care of that many animals properly."

"Well, you can't fault her dedication," I said, trying to be charitable. "I just don't always approve of her tactics."

"She's zealous about saving the wetlands," he agreed. "No question about that. I just hope she doesn't get herself into trouble. Last time she was in here, she was carrying on about land-grabbers and hinting there was evidence that the wetlands might not belong to Costa Bella after all.''

"Have you heard anything like that?" I asked.

He shook his head. ''A company of their standing, I don't think it's real likely they're involved in anything shady. No, I think poor old Mabel's a bit delusional.''

I kept quiet. I wasn't going to let on I might be encouraging those delusions by agreeing to help her out.

While we were talking, the threatened rain had become a reality, and by the time I left, it was pouring hard.

Lumbered with the carrier and trying not to jostle the cat, I made a dash for the station wagon. Thus preoccupied, I wasn't sure if I truly saw or just imagined that someone was watching me from a car parked a little further down the street.

Crouched like a shiny black bug, gleaming in the rain, large sideview mirrors adding to the illusion of a fly poised for take-off, it looked suspiciously like the Volkswagen that had been parked next to mine at the Doggie Diner the other day.

I had the uneasy feeling I was being followed.

· 13 ·

♣ Scatcat ♣

VISIBILITY WAS TOO poor to check for a license plate
or even a bumper sticker, those visual sound bites that
frequently offer insight into a driver's character. With
their pithy observations about causes and issues,
bumper stickers are ideally suited to the California
lifestyle. A kind of mobile soapbox, urging us to Save
the Whales, warning us that Extinction Is Forever,
and reminding us of our Right to Arm Bears.

"I really can't take anyone seriously who chooses
to follow people in a noisy Volkswagen Beetle.
Hardly a low-profile vehicle," I said to Watson who
had clambered over to sniff a welcome to her friend
as soon as I put the carrier in the back of the station
wagon.

Watson responded with a loud sneeze. From the
carrier came an answering moan.

Like me, Watson seemed to have a knack for attracting an odd assortment of acquaintance. In my experience, pets often take on the personalities of their
owners. Take Trixie. Like Tony, she was unpredict-

able, always ready for a lark or a scrap. I was glad I had left her at home, shut in the guest bathroom. She and Hobo were not going to make compatible house-guests.

The rain streamed down, and peer as I might through the hyper windshield wipers, there was no way I could glimpse the VW's driver, never mind tell if it was male or female.

"If I liked this kind of weather, I'd have stayed in England," I grumbled to Watson.

It took me all my skill to manoeuvre the wagon out of the narrow street. The windows steamed from my exertions—I'd never been able to get the hang of the defroster, so rarely did I have occasion to use it— and I had lost sight of the VW well before we reached the intersection with Pacific Coast Highway. The traffic lights swayed dangerously in the wind, and Public Works flood warnings were already in place, evidence of the inadequacy of the southern California drainage system to cope with the inevitable winter rains. Southern Californians must be the only people in the world who are surprised when they get wintry weather in the wintertime.

Nearing home, I relaxed my grip on the steering wheel and thought over Dr. Willie's opinion that it was highly unlikely Costa Bella Enterprises would be engaged in wrong-doing. I was inclined to agree and was already regretting my promise to Mabel. I would end up looking ridiculous. Not too difficult at the best of times, there was no point in courting trouble.

I'd give her a call when I got home and say sorry, but I just didn't have the time.

Shooing Trixie into the hall, I set up a sick bay for Hobo in the guest bathroom. I left him in the carrier while I lined a large cardboard box with towels, cutting out an entrance for easy access. The only small dishes I could find for his kibble and water were from my Wedgewood tea set. I seldom entertained people since Roger died, so why not use bone china for my animal guests? I filled a large baking pan with sand to serve as a litter box. I doubted I'd ever need that again, either. It was a long time since I'd made so much as a Yorkshire pudding.

Meanwhile, Trixie, knowing there was a stranger inside the bathroom, kept up a continuous yapping in protest of being on the wrong side of the door.

I peered in through the carrier's metal gate and was regarded with a hostile stare. Hobo's brutal experience in the leg-hold trap had done nothing to improve his disposition, and he showed no inclination to look kindly upon me, his saviour. It was not going to be an easy relationship. This was no tame kitty cat, but a wild creature, probably born feral and quite content to remain so. The most I could hope for was a distant respect.

I flipped open the carrier latch. Too late I realized that the bathroom door was not securely closed, and at precisely the moment the cat stepped out of the carrier, Trixie nudged the door open. Before I could stop him, the invalid was out of the bathroom, down the hall, and crashing through the living room picture window, not in the least slowed down by, or apparently even aware of, the missing limb. Trixie, in hot pursuit, stopped only on reaching the window. A California dog, she did not care for the rain. Glass was still falling by the time Hobo reached the bushes lining the rear of my back garden, beyond which lay the wetlands.

Ignoring the insistent ringing of the telephone, I returned to the hospital room so tenderly set up just moments earlier, and gazed in dismay at the upturned Wedgewood bowls and roasting pan. Sand and water were scattered in every direction, and Watson and Trixie lost no time in racing to see who could scoff up the most kibble.

My first instinct had been to follow the cat. But in such foul weather it would have been futile, and I knew he would use all his feral wiles to avoid being caught again. I would leave food out for him and trust that hunger would bring him back eventually. Concerned that his wound might become infected, I decided that if he wasn't back within twenty-four hours, I would set out my Havahart trap for him.

The broken window made me feel vulnerable. I should fix that first. But that meant going out to the shed for some plywood. In the rain I really didn't feel that ambitious.

I took a bowl of cat kibble out to the covered back porch. A mockingbird that had been sheltering from the storm flew off at my approach. I was still feeling a little conscience-stricken about that when I heard footsteps on the gravel path. It was my turn to be startled.

A man stood at the kitchen door. He was staring down the path toward the wetlands.

· 14 ·

Gentleman Caller

IT WAS BUD Hefner. "Is your cat all right?" he asked.

His umbrella had not afforded much protection against the storm. Rain dripped from his homburg hat on to the shoulders of his well-tailored winter coat, an outfit strangely out of place here on the West Coast, where people tend to make do with ski jackets to see them through our relatively few days of cold and wet weather.

I urged him to come in from the storm.

"Forgive me if I startled you," he said in that precise manner of his. "I have been ringing the front doorbell for some time. There being no reply, I thought I would try the back door. I knew you were home; your car is in the driveway. Not getting a response, then hearing the sound of breaking glass, I became concerned for your safety."

"That's very kind of you," I said, taking his hat and helping him off with his coat, under which he wore a black pin-stripe suit, white shirt, and black tie.

He carried a plastic grocery bag. "I'm returning

the towel you were so kind as to loan me the other day," he said.

I had forgotten all about the towel, one of several old discards I kept in the car ready for animal emergencies.

It was odd that he would choose such a wretched day to come out, and on such a paltry excuse. I was about to say that he shouldn't have bothered, when Trixie bounded down the hall and greeted him like an old friend, jumping up with unwarranted enthusiasm considering the inconvenience she had put him to.

Watson, on the other hand, chose not to be charmed, and returned his greeting with indifference. She did, however, make a point of jumping into her chair before he had a chance to sit down. Just as well—I'd have hated to see that fine suit covered in dog hair.

Unperturbed by, maybe even unaware of, the slight, Bud Hefner asked what had alarmed the cat. "Did the dogs upset him?"

"You could say that," I said. "But he's feral and not used to being indoors. It didn't take much to set him off."

"I know nothing about wild cats," he said.

"I don't know a whole lot, myself," I said. "Mabel, now, she's the expert."

"Mabel?"

"Mabel Redpath. You must have seen her in the park. She feeds the ferals every night."

"No. I don't believe so."

"Oh, and she was the one who got into a shouting match at the hearing the other evening. Bit of a busy-body she is. Opinions on everything. She's even got a theory about who killed Bill Jackson."

"Really?" He looked surprised. "And what is that?"

Belatedly realizing that I was about to betray a confidence, I abruptly changed the subject.

"Please come and sit down. May I offer you a cup of tea?"

"That would be very welcome, if I'm not keeping you from anything," he said, following me into the sitting-room.

"Actually, in the afternoon I'm usually out checking the shelters, but not in this downpour."

He looked puzzled. "Shelters? For what reason?"

"I'm a pet detective," I explained. "I look for lost pets. Right now I'm trying to find a Puli."

"A Puli? Interesting breed. Descended from the Magyar sheepherding dogs, I believe."

I was impressed. He was the first person not to ask me what a Puli was. "Do you have pets?" I asked.

"No. I have too many allergies," he replied with a rueful smile, adding, "And the cat, is that one of your lost pets also?"

"No. Hobo's a feral cat that had been caught in a steel-jawed trap. I brought him back from the vet's this afternoon." I stepped back into the kitchen to prepare the tea.

"Ah, yes," he said, raising his voice a little to

reach me. "I recall overhearing you telling Amelia about it at the meeting. Setting traps. A cruel and vicious thing to do."

"He's probably headed for the bunker," I said. "That's a favourite haunt of his. He'll find a dry spot. I'll go out there tomorrow and look for him."

"A word of caution," Hefner warned. "Someone may still be setting traps out there. I would hate you to have an accident. Until the authorities put a stop to it, you'd better stay off the wetlands."

"That may take a while," I said. "With Bill Jackson gone, his replacement has to get up to speed. Oh, I'll be careful," I added. How nice to have someone be so solicitous of my welfare.

"Have there been any developments in the case, do you know?" he asked.

I opened a packet of petit beurre biscuits, a favourite of Watson's—a plain English cookie, not too much of an indulgence—and set them out on a plate on the tea tray. Really, if people were going to keep dropping in like this, I'd better brush up on my hostessing skills.

"The police seem to think that Bill's wife Rosemary did it. Which, if you knew them as well as I do, you would know is patently ridiculous. Just because Rosemary was nowhere to be found at the time, they assume she's the murderer."

"It must be very distressing to hear such accusations about your friend," he sympathized.

"She had just left for Europe that morning," I went

on. "The police are trying to locate her right now, to bring her back."

Hefner expressed interest. "Europe? Is she on vacation?"

"I don't think so. I believe this was something that came up unexpectedly. She told a friend of mine that she'd received important news from over there."

I glanced at the clock. "Excuse me. I really ought to ring someone to come and fix the window before it gets too late."

I left him to enjoy his tea, with Trixie cadging tidbits. Watson remained stubbornly aloof on her chair in the kitchen, biscuits notwithstanding. I checked the Yellow Pages and called a couple of local glass repair places. The response was the same in each case. Due to the storm and the lateness of the hour, they wouldn't be able to get out until the following day at the earliest. It all depended on the weather.

Hefner nodded sympathetically. "I'd be happy to help secure the window for the night."

I accepted readily. We took down the drapes, already drenched, and laid them on the damp carpet. Sorting around in the shed, we came up with a couple of panels of plywood, which we propped against the outside of the window.

"I don't guarantee that it's waterproof," he said, helping me sweep up the shards of glass. "But it will keep out the driving rain."

"More to the point, it'll keep the dogs in," I said gratefully. The rain spattered against the panelling, and Watson stirred restlessly in her chair as a particularly strong gust of wind slammed the side gate shut. Bud must have left it unlatched when he came to the back door.

Thanking him again for his kindness and promising to be careful next time I ventured onto the wetlands, I saw him to the door.

Despite the storm, he had walked the few blocks to my house. Not one to be put off by a little rain, I noted appreciatively.

As he turned at the gate to wave, I caught sight of the black Volkswagen as it sped away around the corner.

Before I had a chance to speculate on that, I heard the phone ringing and hurried back in to answer it.

It was Tony. "Where the bloody 'ell are you? I've been ringing all day," he squawked.

Oh dear. Entertaining Bud Hefner had driven all thoughts of Tony from my head.

It was nearly five o'clock, and I didn't know what time the police station closed. Did police stations close? Not so strange a question as one might suppose. My great Aunt Nell, who lives in darkest Sussex, had written not too long ago of a visit to her local constabulary to lodge a complaint about squatters moving into the neighbourhood. She found a sign on the door: Closed for Lunch.

I quickly bundled Trixie and Watson into the car and was halfway to police station before I remembered that in all the excitement, I had quite forgotten to ring Mabel to tell her of my decision not to accept her assignment. But it would soon be dusk. She was probably on her way to feed the ferals by now.

· 15 ·

Trixie Leads the Way

"I'M ONLY A bird in a gilded cage, a bee-yoo-tiful sight to see . . ." The strains of the old English music hall ditty assailed my ears long before I reached the information desk to inquire about Tony's release.

The desk sergeant nodded in the direction of the voice.

"Been like that all day," he said. "He's got quite a repertoire."

"In that case, you'll be glad to see the back of him," I said. "How much?" I was anxious to get out of there and back to the car where I'd left Trixie and Watson. This was the first time I'd left them alone together in a confined space, and I wasn't totally sure I could rely on Watson's good breeding to avoid a fight.

I was directed to a window down the hall, where I paid Tony's bail and took a seat while I awaited his release.

Abruptly, the singing stopped, and soon Tony emerged from a side door further down the corridor.

"Take it easy, Grandpa," said the young desk sergeant kindly, returning the contents of Tony's pockets to him.

Tony swung around and shadow-boxed in what I trusted was mock anger.

" 'Ere, punk. Who're you calling Grandpa?" he said.

Anthony Tipton, alias John B. Bull, had been charged with misdemeanour trespass, a minor offence compared with his lifetime résumé, but one which Tony was determined to make the most of in his efforts to draw attention to his cause.

I grabbed his arm and pulled him away.

"Come along, Tony. We've had enough trouble with the law for one day."

Out of the corner of my eye, I saw Detective Mallory emerge from his office. He hesitated for a moment, as if deliberating whether or not to come over and speak to us. Then, apparently thinking better of it, he walked on down the corridor.

I sighed. Once again, he had observed me at less than my best.

Kept indoors most of the day because of the rain, the dogs needed exercise. The bark park was on our way to where Tony had left his car, so we decided to go there first.

There were only a few other dogs in the bark park, their owners watching them indulgently from nearby benches, like proud parents beside a kiddies' jungle gym.

Trixie and Watson were eager to be in the fenced area where they could safely and legally run off leash. But we were still making our way through the double safety gates when Trixie stopped, raised her nose to catch a scent on the wind, and dashed back out again, headed in the direction of the duck pond.

"Stop her before she gets to the ducks again!" I called, as Tony turned to chase after her.

To my surprise, though, Trixie halted in mid-dash before she reached the pond and started snuffling in the bushes that lined the footpath.

Watson, who had been following at a sedate pace, now stood behind her, very still, in a pointing stance.

"Watch out, Tony," I called, as he approached to investigate. "It might be a skunk."

Undeterred, he pushed aside the lower branches of the shrubbery, preparing to lift Trixie out of there.

He stood up again in a hurry. "What the 'ell!" he said in surprise.

I hurried over.

"Look 'ere," he said.

At first glance I took it to be somebody sleeping, probably one of the homeless people who sought shelter in the park.

I quickly snapped a leash on Watson, then took a closer look.

With growing horror, my eyes took in the mud-spattered sweatpants, the torn jacket, the blood-matted grey hair, the worn tennis shoes with the silver duct tape. A red knit cap lay nearby.

"Poor cow. She's 'ad it, I'm afraid, luv," said Tony, in answer to my protest that she must have fallen and hit her head, that she needed medical attention.

It was dusk, the time that she customarily started her rounds of feeding the feral cats.

But no cats would be fed tonight.

Mabel Redpath would make the six o'clock news at last.

· 16 ·

♣ ♣

Crime Scene

I STAYED WITH Mabel and the dogs while Tony ran to the Doggie Diner to call 911. Soon the wail of police sirens filled the damp evening air.

If there was one thing I was sure of, it was that curiosity had killed the cat caretaker. As I looked at Mabel's pathetic figure lying facedown, her blood mingling with the mud, my attention was caught by a piece of paper sticking out of her jacket pocket. Before I could stop them, my fingers seemed to take on a mind of their own, and filched the paper before the words "tampering with evidence" even entered my head.

Conscience-stricken, I took a quick look at my swag, then breathed a sigh of relief. It was only the pet classifieds from the *Surf City News*. Nothing the police would be interested in.

I stuffed the clipping into my pocket as Officer Offley came plodding down the path, his manner no warmer than it had been at Bill Jackson's house the other day. He regarded Tony and me with disapproval, ready, I was quite sure, to believe the worst of us.

He produced notebook and pen and asked gruffly, "Who discovered the body?"

Something about the man never failed to annoy me. If he expected the worst of me, I was ready to oblige.

"Trixie," I said.

"Trixie who?"

"Trixie Tipton."

He looked around and, seeing no other female in evidence, asked "Where is she?" with a puzzled look on his doughy face.

I pointed down at the little terrier sniffing his trouser leg with interest.

Offley was not amused. "Mrs. Doolittle, this is a serious business," he said, moving out of Trixie's range.

Tony was about to say something, but Offley rebuffed him with "I'll get to you later." Then, turning back to me, Offley said, "Now, where were we?"

"You asked who discovered the body. I told you. Mr. Tipton and I were walking our dogs, Trixie ran ahead and started snuffling in the bushes, and . . ."

"Then Tipton discovered the body?"

"In a manner of speaking."

This exchange was mercifully cut short by the arrival of Detective Mallory. He took in the scene with an expert glance, then turned his attention to the body.

"Any sign of the weapon?" he asked Offley.

"No, sir. Probably some kind of blunt instrument. The men are looking for it now."

Mallory nodded. "Identity?" he asked.

"People here claim it's a Mabel Redpath," said Offley.

"Not 'a Mabel Redpath'," I said. "It is Mrs. Mabel Redpath. Kindly have a little more respect."

Never having particularly cared for Mabel alive, I was surprised to find myself defending her in death.

"Mrs. Doolittle. You again," said Mallory drily, apparently only now becoming aware of my presence.

Offley turned to Tony. "Now, Mr. Tipton, what is your interest in the deceased?" he asked.

"Interest? Do I have to have an interest? It's a bloody public park."

"Anyway," I put in, "Mr. Tipton was arrested yesterday morning and has only just been released from jail, within the past hour or so. I believe you will find the time of Mrs. Redpath's death to have been . . ."

Offley glowered at me. "When I want your statement, I'll ask for it," he said with uncalled-for boorishness.

Turning back to Tony, he said, "There are numerous witnesses who can testify they saw you quarreling with the deceased at City Hall recently."

"But I bloody called you," said Tony.

"Could be a ruse," said Offley.

With what I considered admirable restraint, Tony simply threw up his hands in exasperation.

Meanwhile, a veritable posse of official vehicles

had arrived on the scene, variously labeled Crime Scene, Ambulance, and Coroner, dispensing an astonishing array of people bearing yellow tape, notebooks, cameras, plastic gloves, and a considerable amount of other unidentifiable but, I'm sure, essential paraphernalia.

And just in case we wanted to know, these people all wore jackets with the names of their departments stencilled on the back. Official California seems excessively fond of labeling itself, though for whose benefit it might be I'm at a loss to imagine, since they must all know each other pretty well to judge from the goings-on around me.

Watson, ever the soul of discretion, stood quietly by my side, studying each new arrival with guarded curiosity. Trixie, on the other hand, dashed in and out among a smorgasbord of trouser legs, a diversion which Tony didn't seem particularly interested in discouraging.

To add to the confusion, the rain had come on in earnest, dripping heavily from the trees and pinging off the empty cat food tins. We were all getting wetter by the minute.

A youth of about seventeen years old who, from his uniform, I took to be a police cadet, produced an umbrella and attempted to shelter Mallory as the detective strode about the scene.

"I want an approximate time of death as soon as possible," said Mallory to the man from the coroner's office.

"She's been here about twenty-four hours," I said.

Mallory turned to me with something like astonishment on his usually impassive countenance.

"What makes you say that?" he asked.

"The empty cat food tins. Mabel always comes here around this time in the evening to feed the ferals. If she had recently arrived, the tins would still be full. Possibly she wouldn't even have opened them yet. The cats won't come out until after dark."

Mallory jotted something in his notebook but made no further comment, merely nodding an indication to the coroner's assistant that he get on with his job.

From what I could overhear, Offley was now of the opinion that Mabel was the victim, if not of Tony, then of a random mugging, the area being a known hang-out for vagrants.

Mallory listened intently, but kept his own counsel. I felt I ought to tell him about Mabel's suspicions. She knew the people who called the park home, sometimes feeding them as well as the cats. I doubted very much if one of them would have harmed her. A reference to her as a "crazy old broad" would be as far as their belligerence went.

There was something more sinister afoot here than a mugging, and I felt it was my duty to speak up. But I hesitated, not wishing to appear captious. I had already been snubbed once.

Finally I said, "I think it has something to do with the controversy over the wetlands."

Mallory turned cool blue-grey eyes in my direction.

The chill wind ruffled his thick grey hair over his forehead, and he ran his hand through it impatiently.

"What have you been doing, Mrs. Doolittle? Reading your tea-leaves? Perhaps the rest of us should go home and leave you to solve the crime. But please, go on."

"I know for a fact that Mabel was on to something. She told me . . ."

"Told you what?"

Come to think of it, she hadn't told me much at all. Certainly nothing that she hadn't shared with all and sundry over the past few weeks. I was the one who was supposed to come up with the evidence. Suddenly I felt uncomfortable acknowledging that I had offered to help her. No point in bringing that up now. Mabel was dead; so was the assignment, in effect.

"Well, it was common knowledge that she suspected the people at Costa Bella Enterprises of some kind of wrong-doing, and she claimed to have evidence to support her suspicions," I covered lamely.

"Mrs. Doolittle, I don't have time to stand here listening to warmed-over gossip," he said in exasperation and turned his attention back to the crime scene.

That stung. When would I learn to keep my mouth shut?

Tony made matters worse by leaping to my defense.

"Leave it out, mate," he said to Mallory in an

overly familiar tone. "Delilah here's just lost a good friend. She don't need no bleeding third degree."

Offley placed a warning hand on Tony's arm.

Tony shrugged him off angrily. Trixie, sniffing at Offley's trouser leg and sensing the hostility in his tone, snapped aggressively and started yapping. Offley made as if to kick the little dog away.

Tony gave the policeman a shove, and the next thing anybody knew Tony was being arrested for interfering with an officer in the performance of his duty.

I started to protest, but soon had my hands full trying to get hold of Trixie who was attempting to follow Tony into the patrol car.

With Trixie firmly under control at last I waited, uncertain of what to do next.

That dilemma was solved when the umbrella carrier headed in my direction.

"Detective Mallory says you can go," he said. "He'll contact you later about your statement. Says you can take the umbrella."

Though it was quite a way through the park back to my car, I declined the umbrella, a gesture I almost immediately regretted as possibly being perceived as ungracious. But with two dogs to cope with, my hands were already full.

I waved good-bye to Tony, sitting forlornly in the back of the patrol car, waiting to be hauled off to the nick again. He gave a helpless shrug. But at least he knew Trixie would be taken care of.

Three very muddy individuals climbed into the station wagon. It was useless to try to dry off the dogs. Watson I could have handled, but after standing about for a couple of hours, I was too tired and discouraged to tackle Trixie. What were a few muddy paw prints between friends?

Trixie, somewhat subdued by the unexpected turn of events, sought comfort from Tony's jacket which lay on the backseat where he had tossed it when we went for a walk.

Watson sat in front, her weight leaning against me, offering comfort and warmth.

"I feel dreadful for not taking Mabel seriously," I told her. "No matter what the police think, this was no random mugging."

I went over my recent conversations with Mabel. She had proof at her house, she'd said, but the cat had peed on it.

Disagreeable as it sounded, I had to get my hands on that proof.

. 17 .

The Cat's Meow

No BARKING HERALDED my approach to Mabel's
house. That, and the yellow tape across the front
porch announcing Police Line Do Not Cross in large
black letters, told me that Surf City's finest had already been by.

On entering the house to a rush of dogs and cats,
the police would have immediately contacted animal
control. Mabel's pets would have been taken to the
shelter where they would be cared for until relatives
could be contacted.

It was the morning after our dismal discovery at
the bark park. Though the rain had finally quit, the
sky remained gunmetal sullen, threatening more later.

In an attempt to be inconspicuous, I was wearing
neutral colours: tan anorak, shirt, jeans, and desert
boots. In California's winter it is advisable to dress
in layers. A cool morning can be followed by afternoon temperatures in the eighties.

I had walked the few blocks to Mabel's house. A
one-level, ranch-style, it was in one of the many sub-

divisions that had sprung up mushroomlike in the fifties and sixties to house the employees of southern California's blossoming aerospace industry. Thirty years later, these homes afforded incredibly low mortgage payments for older residents like Mabel and the Jacksons, two houses down.

I looked hopefully for signs of Rosemary's return as I passed her driveway and was struck again by the coincidence of the homes being so close and their owners both the victims of recent and violent death. That the two murders were related, I had no doubt. But even if, in the extremely unlikely case that Rosemary had killed her husband in a fit of marital strife—a theory Detective Mallory seemed bent on proving—there could be absolutely no reason why she would have killed Mabel. Unless she had succumbed to that same urge to throttle the exasperating woman that I myself had been obliged to suppress on more than one occasion.

Such speculations were abruptly dismissed as I came to grips with the more immediate problem of how to get into Mabel's house.

Unwilling to defy the yellow tape in broad daylight, I walked on down the block, around the corner, to the alley that ran along the rear of the houses. The latch to Mabel's back gate gave easily, and I walked quickly through the overgrown backyard to the kitchen door, the six-foot redwood fence separating the houses conveniently shielding me from the prying eyes of any nosey neighbour who might be watching.

The kitchen door was locked.

I looked around for another means of entry. What Mabel had called the cattery, actually an enclosed porch running across the rear of the house, offered a possibility. The screen door resisted at first, but it wasn't locked, just stiff from the metal frame being warped and rusted from the sea air. One good shove and I was in.

I stood for a moment on the faded blue indoor-outdoor carpet while I got my bearings. The stale odour of litter boxes, a scatter of dishes, some still partially filled with kibble, and a variety of cat beds of every shape, material, and colour, recalled the recent occupants.

It was so quiet. No barking dogs jostling each other to greet me, no cats gazing with curious eyes from every available vantage point.

The eerie silence was broken by a crash of something, perhaps pottery or glass, hitting the kitchen floor.

Someone else was in the house. I held my breath and listened. For what? Footsteps? An angry expletive? A police command? I heard nothing but the thudding of my own heart.

As I stood there listening, I was startled again by something rubbing against my leg. It was a long-haired calico, no doubt an escapee from animal control's round-up. I breathed a sigh of relief. She must have caused the crash.

"Naughty puss," I said to the pretty orange, white,

and black cat. ''You gave me such a scare. What did you break?''

I picked her up and went into the kitchen to investigate. Pieces of what appeared to have been a glass fruit bowl littered the floor.

''Clumsy little thing,'' I scolded. ''How did you manage to do that?''

I stifled the impulse to clean up the mess. It wouldn't do to leave any incriminating evidence around from which the police could draw yet another wrong conclusion.

A small wooden desk stood against one wall. Alongside the telephone was a pile of classified ''free to you'' ads, and a clipboard holding Mabel's Neighbourhood Watch notes—a perfect foil for her prying eyes. Well, who was prying now? Not me, I reassured myself. Mine was a healthy curiosity, in a good cause. Nevertheless, maybe some people wouldn't see it that way. Detective Mallory, for instance. The thought made me quicken my search for the missing document Mabel had referred to. Best get out of there as soon as possible.

On the floor beside the desk stood a stack of scrapbooks. They seemed all to contain newspaper clippings about Surf City and its residents for the past several decades. Why would Mabel keep all this stuff? She was either a historian or a pack rat. I opted for the latter.

I imagined her sitting here working the ads, making telephone calls, in a never-ending endeavour to save unwanted animals. A thought occurred. Was it from here also she made threatening telephone calls? I pulled open a drawer and found a stack of bills awaiting payment. I opened the telephone bill and scanned the listings. Only two long distance calls, both to Evie's number.

A plastic grocery bag stood on the kitchen counter, containing a dozen or so tins of cat food. I snapped one open and emptied the contents into one of many clean plastic dishes piled in the sink. I filled another with fresh water and returned with both dishes to the cattery, the calico meowing by my side.

Now, where might Mabel have put an important, but cat-soiled piece of paper? She wouldn't necessarily have hidden it. She'd never indicated that she had any sense of being in danger. She had put it outside to dry, she'd said. I glanced through the porch screen to the backyard. I couldn't see anywhere she might safely have left an important document. And with the weather so uncertain of late, she wouldn't have risked it getting wet again or blowing away.

Maybe she considered the cattery to be "outside". If so, the paper would have to be somewhere the cats couldn't get at it again.

The calico, having eaten her fill, was exercising her claws on a tall cat tree that stood in the far corner of the porch, it's carpet covering shredded nearly bare in some areas. The top shelf was almost flush with the ceiling, leaving no room for a cat to alight. The calico had now climbed the tree and was pawing at a piece of paper resting on the top shelf.

"What've you got there, miss?" I said, pushing her away. She jumped down with a protesting meow. Standing on the bottom shelf of the tree, I reached up and pulled out a faded yellow newspaper clipping. A faint smell of ammonia still clung to it.

Was this what I was looking for? An old article from the *Surf City News*? I barely had time to catch more than a glimpse of the date and read something about a Spanish land grant, when I became aware of movement behind me. Someone pushed me in the small of my back, and the paper was snatched out of my hand.

I fell forward onto the cat tree, and was still picking myself up, when I heard the front door slam, soon followed by the sound of a car engine starting up and driving off—a sound which, even to my untrained ear, had the distinctive character of a Volkswagen.

So it wasn't the cat that had knocked over the glass bowl. It was an intruder. An intruder? Wasn't that a case of the pot calling the kettle black?

I shuddered. I might have been the killer's next victim.

"All the more reason to get to the bottom of this," I told the calico.

I ran out the kitchen door, alongside the house to the driveway. I was too late to confirm my suspicions, but just in time to see a police patrol car cruising toward the house.

· 18 ·

Oddly Enough

I STEPPED BACK out of sight and watched as the patrol car drove on by, coming to a stop at the Jackson house. Then I slipped back down the side of the house, through the gate, into the alley, and headed for home, relieved to have escaped being caught in a situation I would have been hard-pressed to talk myself out of.

Back home, I stopped only long enough to check on Watson and Trixie before heading out again. I had forgotten to put Watson's blue Teddy bear away, out of Trixie's reach. Watson tolerated Trixie to a point; that point was Teddy. I had tried to distract Trixie with her own toys, but she had taken a fancy to the blue bear. As soon as I got in I saw that it was in Trixie's basket. Both dogs looked on anxiously as I put Teddy away in a cupboard, there to stay until our tiresome house-guest had gone.

I checked for messages, hoping for something on the Puli. Nothing. Next I tried calling Mr. Glass, the window repairman. All I got was his voice mail:

"Auto glass, press 1; mirrors, press 2;" and so on. I pressed 3, for windows, and we began again: *"Business, press 1; residence, press 2."* I pressed 2. *"Please hold and your call will be answered in the order received."* I hung up in disgust. I'd call back when I had more time. There'd been no earthquakes recently; did they really expect me to believe there were that many broken mirrors and windows in Surf City? We were in for a ton of bad luck if that was the case. More likely, the one and only Mr. Glass was out on the one and only job of the day and would call me as soon as he came home for lunch.

I checked the back porch to see if Hobo had returned. The kibble remained untouched. There was little point in searching for him. Cats, even domesticated ones, are notoriously hard to find if they don't want to be found. As for ferals, well, don't even bother. I was reminded of Kipling's "He went through the wet wild woods, waving his wild tail, and walking by his wild lone. But he never told anybody." Hobo was out there walking, or limping, through the wild wetlands, and he certainly wasn't going to tell me where he was.

ENTERING THE OFFICE of the weekly *Surf City News* was like stepping into the past. The pungent smell of printer's ink and the jangling doorbell announcing my arrival both recalled local newspaper offices of an earlier time.

Behind the heavily polished wooden counter, Ed

Fellowes, owner and editor-in-chief, crouched over an old Royal manual typewriter, pecking away like some particularly cantankerous secretary bird.

He pushed the green eye-shade back over his thinning grey hair and squinted at me through gold-rimmed spectacles perched on the end of his thin, hawklike nose.

"Can I help you, miss?"

The "miss" notwithstanding, I was shocked that he didn't recognize me. It was a few months since I had last seen him, and I had heard that he was in failing health, but I hadn't realized just how frail and forgetful he had become.

In a world of computer-driven communications, Ed Fellowes was an anachronism. His weekly newspaper long ago overtaken by the big metropolitan dailies, he nevertheless kept to the leisurely pace that had sustained him for half a century and still painstakingly set the news on an old Linotype machine.

That the paper continued to exist was due almost entirely to the efforts of his chief, and only, reporter, his daughter Lily, who virtually ran the paper single-handedly. In this she was supported by the loyalty of local readers, who could still rely on the *News* for information about the things that really mattered: the births and deaths, weddings and anniversaries, of their friends and neighbours; the tide tables, and the fishing reports. But as the older generation declined, so did the paper's circulation, and it was only a matter of time before the paper would fold. Lily had already confided to me that once her father passed away, she would close up shop.

"But not until then," she had said. "Take the paper away, and he'd shrivel up like an old leaf." From all appearances, that day was not too far off.

A copy of the latest edition lay on the counter. It had been a big week for news. The lead story reported Bill Jackson's murder. The Coastal Commission hearing shared top-of-the-page honours. Below the fold, Tony's exploits were featured: "Local surfer battles tidal inlet." Lily had a soft spot for Tony, and he came off well in the article.

Lily came out to the lobby when she heard the doorbell, closing the door of the printing room behind her, muffling the sound of the presses. She was a heavy-set, good-natured woman, whose warm personality would have served her well during her years as a top reporter on a Chicago daily. She had given up that promising career a few years ago, after her husband passed away and she moved back to Surf City to help her widowed father.

She chose comfort over style, and today was wearing a long, full wool skirt in a muted plaid, a matching oversized blouse, and a Paisley scarf knotted around her neck. Her dark grey hair was shaped close to her head, and her cheeks were flushed, no doubt from the exertion of wrestling with the ancient presses.

"Delilah!" she greeted. "Got an item for the lost and found column?"

I have to confess, I seldom used the classified pages in my friend's newspaper anymore. The circulation was so low, I got better results from the large county daily and the *Los Angeles Times*.

"Not today. Something quite different. But I'm hoping you can help me."

"We'll try, won't we, Dad?"

Ed snorted disinterest and returned to his type-writer.

"It's a bit of a puzzle, actually," I went on, belatedly realizing that I should have concocted some plausible explanation of why I was there looking for a newspaper item of half a century ago. "I was wondering if I might take a look at some back issues."

"Of course," she said.

"You have them on microfilm?"

"Only since the sixties. Didn't think there'd be much call for them before that."

The disappointment must have shown on my face, because she went on. "We still have most of the original papers before that. At least back to the forties, when Dad first bought the paper after he got out of the service. He didn't have the heart to throw them out. So sentimental about the paper, he is." She smiled at her father fondly. "What date were you interested in?"

Lifting the counter flap, she led the way into the musty storeroom which served as a library. She reached up and pulled on a string, and a single low-watt bulb, swinging in its metal shade, illuminated the room, lighting up first one wall then the other, finally coming to rest to light the center of the room, where stood a desk, a chair, and a wooden step stool.

"Will you be all right here by yourself?" Lily asked. "I have to keep an eye on Dad. He makes so many mistakes these days."

"Don't let me keep you," I said, relieved. I didn't want her looking over my shoulder. I would be hard put to explain just what I was looking for.

"Don't play with matches," she said with an easy laugh as she left.

My eyes gradually became accustomed to the poor light. Three walls held long racks where newspapers hung on wooden binders. The dates, some nearly illegible, were scribbled in faded ink on labels attached to the spines. Many of the labels were torn, and several of the binders were out of order. The earlier editions, from the forties and fifties, were jammed on the top row, and I had to use the step stool to reach them.

I located the binder for the three months from June to August 1946, and tugged it out in a cloud of dust. This was probably the first time these newspapers had been disturbed since they had been placed here originally. Mabel's scrapbooks were probably the only other repository of such information extant.

In earlier, more prosperous times, the paper had been a robust sixteen or twenty pages, more during the holiday sales, compared to the eight pages it was reduced to these days.

Turning the fragile pages, I was sidetracked, fascinated by old photographs, advertisements, prices. I closed my eyes and tried to visualize the date I had seen when the clipping was snatched out of my hand. I knew I had the year right, but I wasn't sure of the month. Was it June or July?

I found what I was looking for in the edition for the last week of July. The article told of old Spanish land grants, deeds, and conveyances—none of which appeared, to my untutored eye at least, to shed much light on the current wetlands controversy. I made some notes and was closing the binder when, as the pages started to fan through my fingers, my attention was caught by another, far more interesting story on the reverse page. It was an account of the disappearance of Rosemary's sister Valerie. The article was accompanied by a photograph of her distraught fiancé, Bud Hefner.

Bud Hefner! This was news, indeed. To me, anyway. Rosemary had never mentioned that our local war hero had been her sister's fiancé. But then, she had seldom mentioned her sister at all, and I had not wanted to pry.

Lily's voice brought me back to the present with a start. "You've been quiet as a mouse in here. Did you find what you were looking for?" she asked. Then, her eyes falling on the page I had been reading, continued, "The Jackson story. So sad. And now Bill's been killed, and Rosemary nowhere to be found." She shook her head. "That family seems doomed."

She smoothed the brittle newsprint with her hand, folding back an errant corner. "Poor Valerie. The police suspected foul play, but they never had any firm leads. I was just a kid at the time, but I remember Mom warning me not to talk to strangers. Put the fear of God in me."

Ed, who had followed his daughter into the storeroom, joined in the conversation. "Old Bud was never the same after that," he croaked, displaying the uncanny ability of the elderly to recall totally events that happened fifty years ago, while often unable to remember what happened last week. "Just got out of the service, both of us. Me in the Pacific, him in Europe."

His eyes dimmed at the recollection. "We used to be the best of pals, but her running off like that seemed to turn him in on himself. He was left all alone. No family to fall back on. Bud, he blamed it on what happened to his face. See, he was a handsome fellow before a German mine got him . . ."

"I can't say I entirely blame her," said Lily. "Young girl like that probably couldn't handle it, the terrible disfigurement. But it's been hard on her family. She should have let Rosemary know where she was."

Lily helped me to shove the heavy binder back in its place on the rack, there to remain undisturbed for another few decades, most likely. I was relieved that out of politeness she controlled her journalist's instinct to probe into why I was so interested in that particular story.

I would have been at a loss for an explanation, in any case. What possible interest could the old news clipping have for the driver of the Volkswagen? Or for anyone else, come to that?

But it was clear that it meant something to somebody. Mabel had known or guessed what that something was. And had paid for it with her life.

• 19 •
Even Oddlier

WITH MUCH TO occupy my mind, I crossed Main Street to Amber's Beauty Connection. I was to meet Evie at the Coastal Commission hearing in Long Beach that evening, and I was determined to get my hair done before undergoing her scrutiny once more.

A few tourists had braved the drizzle and were browsing the surf shops and funky souvenir establishments that graced our main thoroughfare near the pier, buying postcards and gifts to prove to distant friends that they had indeed reached our fabled shores. A wet suit–clad surfer strode by barefoot, surfboard under his arm, arousing variously admiring, curious, or envious glances from some of the younger tourists.

The rain made no difference to surfers. It was just as wet in as out, and the surf was often at its best during a storm. Tony, back in the arms of the law, would regret missing some good waves.

From Tony my thoughts turned to Trixie and Watson, perforce left at home for the afternoon. I didn't like leaving them to their own devices for any length of time.

I voiced my concern to Amber, eyeing me critically as she hovered over my head with scissors and comb.

"I hope this isn't going to take too long," I said.

"Well, if you will only come in once in a blue moon, I can't be expected to work miracles in half an hour," she huffed, implying that it would indeed take a miracle to make a silk purse out of this particular sow's ear.

I settled on a haircut and set, with a colour rinse for good measure, hoping that the professionally applied variety would have better results than my earlier self-inflicted attempt.

While she worked, Amber asked, in the manner of beauticians the world over, how things were going, prepared to be mother confessor, therapist, or counsellor as circumstances required. But nothing that I could divulge compared with the conversation at the next station.

". . . the four thousand I gave her for a nose job . . . never got that back," the customer was saying in a voice loud enough to be heard throughout the salon.

While these confidences were being revealed, the operator was doing something quite extraordinary to her client's hair—wrapping pieces of aluminum foil randomly throughout her thick, grey locks. It looked quite alarming and one could only pray she wouldn't be struck by lightning before the whole process was completed.

". . . then his Disability ran out . . ." the client continued, as snippets of gossip and hair fell about the room with equal abandon.

Amber and I had to tear ourselves away to go to the shampoo bowl, and by the time we got back it was obvious we had missed some essential thread to the story as the customer, now a recycler's treasure trove of aluminum foil, was saying,

". . . and she said she didn't know who the baby's father was."

"Did she have the baby after she was institutionalized?" her hairdresser wanted to know. So did I. Alas, the answer was lost in the roar of the blow dryer above my head.

"And then the father showed up, and he wanted it," was the last I heard of this fascinating saga.

Really. I should have my hair done more often. Amber continued to brush and blow, unperturbed, as one who has heard it all before.

I gradually gave myself over to her ministrations and let my mind drift. All this talk of missing fathers, plastic surgery, institutions, and Disability checks was stirring some disturbing notions in my head.

Amber's voice brought me out of my reverie. "Did you want spray on that?"

A MOST INFORMATIVE day, I thought, as I made my way home.

I toyed with the idea of passing my suspicions along to Detective Mallory but decided he was overworked enough as it was, with two murders on his hands, and would not care to be burdened with any more of my outlandish theories. A decision I was destined to regret before the week was out.

❖ 20 ❖

Reading Tea-Leaves

IT WAS A relief upon arriving home to find Tony's classic Woody station wagon in the driveway, his surfboard sticking out the back window. Trixie would soon be off my hands.

Tony was sitting on the front step.

"I called you," he said rather accusingly, I thought, as he followed me into the house. "But you wasn't 'ome, so I 'ad one of me mates pick me up."

I might have inquired why he didn't call on said mates more frequently, instead of constantly burdening me with his problems, but I had more pressing questions.

"I thought you were a suspect in Mabel's murder," I said.

"Turns out you were right about the time of the poor old dear's death," he chuckled. "That's when I was in the clink for the bulldozer lark, so I couldn't 'ave done it."

He leaned over to pet Trixie who, ecstatic at his return, was dancing circles around his legs.

"Come on then," he said, tapping his knees. The little dog leapt into his arms.

"Did you miss yer old dad, then?" he said, fondling her head. Trixie licked his face adoringly in answer.

"As for that other business in the park," he said, turning his attention to me again, "they let me off with a caution. Too busy with all these bloody murders to be bovvered with the likes of me."

While he talked, I plugged in the electric kettle and prepared the tea tray. Tony never turned down a cup of tea, and as for myself, I was gasping for one after my exhausting afternoon at the beauty parlour.

Tony looked around the kitchen inquiringly.

"Got any biscuits?" he asked, eyeing a large tin of Peak Frean's, all Scottie dogs and tartan, a recent gift from my great aunt Nell in England who delighted in sending me what she called "reverse CARE packages". I offered Tony the tin, hoping that he wouldn't scoff the lot before I had a chance to sample them.

"Ta, luv," he said, taking one of my favourite bourbons and breaking it into pieces for Trixie. Then, "You bin messin' about with yer 'air again?"

"A trip to the hairdresser's. Do you approve?"

It was incredible the effect my friends' scrutiny of my appearance was having on me these days. I was rather afraid my sensitivity to their remarks dated from my recent reacquaintance with Detective Mallory.

"I suppose it's all right for a change," he said grudgingly.

Well, this was a fine augury of the anticipated appraisal by Evie. I changed the subject.

"Did you know that Bud Hefner was engaged to Rosemary's sister before she disappeared in 1946?" I asked him.

"Getaway. That was before my time. Tell you what, though. I've always thought there was something a bit dodgy about that bloke. The way he keeps to hisself."

That was unfair. "Maybe you'd be cagey if your face was scarred like that."

"Well, I think it's right peculiar that Rosemary's never heard from her sister in all these years." He poured some tea in a saucer and put it down for Trixie. "Maybe he done 'er in."

"What a dreadful thing to say!" I protested.

"How'd you find out about it, anyway?" he asked.

I told him about my visit to Mabel's, and finding the old newspaper clipping.

"You better watch out. You go poking your nose where it don't belong, and next thing you know, it'll be me bailing *you* out the nick."

Perish the thought.

He stood up. "Well, I'm off," he said, gulping down the last of his tea. "Can't stay 'ere chatting all night. Thanks for taking care of Trix. I know you'll always treat 'er right."

He picked up Trixie's empty food dish and took

her leash from the hook by the kitchen door. "Can't be too careful, you know," he added, as if struck by a sudden thought. "Me mate was telling me about some cove over Westgrove way who's been picking up people's dogs, then watching the lost and founds, and collecting the reward. Nothing big, mind you, not enough to alert the police, but he's been making beer money. Thought you might be interested, seeing as how you're in the same line of business, so to speak."

He was gone before I could debate the merits of that last remark. But it was something to keep in mind, as I continued my search for Mariah—a search, I reminded myself, that had been sorely neglected the past couple of days.

I would ring Tony later on and ask if he could give me any more information on the "cove".

I finished my tea and, recalling Mallory's cutting remark about tea-leaves, swirled the dregs in the bottom of the cup, then dumped them into the saucer to form a pattern.

"You're going on a journey," my mother would say. Or, "There's money" or "a handsome stranger, coming into your life."

Right then I'd have settled for a shaggy black Puli.

. 21 .

Battle at the Bunker

THE COASTAL COMMISSION hearing in Long Beach
had dragged on past midnight, offering much the
same arguments, though none of the histrionics, that
had enlivened our Surf City meeting. Evie and I had
left before the meeting was over, leaving Howard to
drive back to the Beverly Bayside Club alone later.
Evie would spend the night with me.

Driving home she complained of the "sheer ennui,
sweetie" of the hearings they had attended over the
past two weeks.

"Not that bad, surely?" I said.

"Much worse, actually. Pure tedium," she replied.
"Honestly, I fail to see what the problem is. No one
seems to understand that once the wetlands are gone,
they are absolutely irreplaceable." She paused to
draw on the pink Sabranie balanced delicately from a
long, tortoiseshell cigarette holder. "Mind you, I'm
all for making a profit at the right time and place.
After all, where would Howard be, not to mention
moi, without it?"

Where indeed? But a nodded agreement was all I could manage. The drive took all my concentration. During the evening, a dense fog had rolled in across the marsh, and the usually fast stretch of Pacific Coast Highway between Long Beach and Surf City, with the wetlands on our left and the Pacific ocean on our right, was reduced to a risky crawl.

Watson, sensing my uneasiness, had roused herself from the back of the wagon and was resting her chin on my shoulder, seeming to peer with me through the fog. Chamois was curled up asleep on Evie's lap.

The fog lifted a little as we approached the entrance to the wetlands interpretive center. During the day I would often pull off here hoping to catch a glimpse of one of the rare white pelicans that were making a comeback, or to spot a blue heron standing motionless in the reeds. Sheer habit made me glance in that direction now. I certainly didn't expect to see anything as the fog drifted in patches across the marsh.

But see something I did. About a quarter of a mile inland, where the bunker was located, I saw a light.

I turned into the gravel parking lot and onto the unpaved access road leading across the marsh toward the bunker, studiously ignoring the Official Vehicles Only Beyond This Point sign.

"Dee! What in heaven's name are you doing? Where are you going?" shrieked Evie.

"There's somebody at the bunker. Probably setting another trap. I've got to stop them. Hobo is out there."

"Hobo?" she asked, clutching the armrest as the wagon jolted across the rutted roadway. "Another of your eccentric coterie?"

"You know. The cat in the trap. I told you about him."

"The last thing you want to do is mess with someone who would set those ugly things," said Evie. "I insist you turn around right now. It's too dangerous."

"If I go back, he'll get away. I've got to find out who it is."

"Well, I'm not sure that I want to. Can't we just call for help? Where's your cell phone?" she said, looking around the car.

"I don't have one."

"Don't have a cell phone! Why ever not?"

"Oh, I don't know, Evie," I sighed, wearying of her protests. "Probably something to do with money."

"Well, this is ridiculous."

Though not ready to admit it, I was beginning to think she might be right.

Not wishing to alert whoever was at the bunker, I had turned off my headlights, making it difficult to see the road ahead. The old station wagon was no off-road vehicle, and it bumped along in a most alarming manner, cat traps and catch poles rattling in the back.

The inevitable happened. I missed a curve and the wagon veered off the narrow path into the marsh.

In vain I spun the wheels, but we just sank deeper into the mud.

"We're stranded," wailed Evie. "Dee, you are the absolute limit."

"If you hadn't distracted me with your whining, I wouldn't have missed the path," I said, perhaps unfairly. "We'll have to go on foot from here. It's not far."

"I'm not going anywhere," Evie stated flatly.

"Stay in the car, then. You'll be perfectly safe."

I took the smaller of the two flashlights I always carry with me, snapped the leash on Watson's collar, and with more bravado than I actually felt, stepped out of the car, immediately sinking ankle deep into the ooze.

Recovering my balance, I sloshed to the road and, with a puzzled but unquestioning Watson by my side, headed for the bunker.

Had I known what I was in for that night, I would have dressed accordingly, but in honour of Evie and my new hair-do (to which, incidentally, Evie had made no reference at all) I had taken extra pains with my appearance. At the very least I would have worn sensible shoes with my pale green jersey wool frock, instead of the strappy heels now slip-sliding under my feet.

The bunker, which by day had appeared to be just an uninteresting mound of earth-covered concrete, took on sinister proportions at night.

The chances were that the trap-setter, if indeed that's who it was, would have taken off at the first sign of our arrival. But if he had set a trap, I had to find it and spring it before Hobo or some other creature got caught.

I stiffened as I heard a slight noise.

"Hobo," I whispered. Not that he knew his name, or would have responded if he did.

I felt a tap on my shoulder. Fear telegraphed an unfamiliar prickling sensation to my arm-pits, and I dropped Watson's leash in alarm.

I turned, shining the flashlight in the face of my assailant, hoping to gain some advantage.

"Do you mind," said Evie. "That light's blinding me."

"Why didn't you say something?" I demanded.

"I didn't want to scare you."

"I thought you were going to wait in the car!"

"I didn't like being out there alone. You were taking far too long. Besides, I thought you might need this to catch the cat with." She was carrying the catch pole.

"I've got to find him first," I said drily, then continued. "Well, now you're here, you can help me look for a trap. It'll be somewhere around here, if there is one."

"What shall I do if I find it?"

"Spring it with that pole. Once it's snapped shut, it will be harmless. But for heaven's sake be careful."

"Make sure Watson doesn't find it first, then."

Watson had wandered off. Maybe she'd found Hobo.

"Watson!" I called loudly, emboldened by Evie's company.

The heavy door of the bunker stood ajar. I pushed it open further and shone the flashlight around. In a far corner, Watson was digging furiously.

"Watson," I said. "Sometimes I wish you'd leave your nose at home," I sighed. "Come here, girl." But Watson stood her ground, pointing at the spot where she had been digging.

At first all I could see was a few bones, which I took to be of some animal that had passed that way long ago. But on closer inspection I saw a skull, not of a fox or a coyote, but undoubtedly of a human. The earth was soft, and the grave looked deeper than Watson could have accomplished in the few minutes she'd been there.

The horror of the discovery soon gave way to the remembrance that an Indian burial site was said to be hereabouts.

"Naughty girl, Watson. Desecrating a grave."

"Evie," I called. "Bring your flashlight in here."

There was no reply. I could hear nothing but the night sounds of the marsh: water lapping, frogs croaking in chorus.

Then I heard a noise coming from near the door and called over my shoulder, "Evie. Come and see what Watson has found."

Watson gave a low warning growl, then a yelp. I was hit from behind. The flashlight dropped from my hand as I fell foward into the grave, but in its wavering light I saw a man with a balaclava over his face, only the eyes uncovered. As he raised his arm to hit me again, there was an unholy feline howl, as some devil cat flew through the air and landed on my assailant's head.

There was a muffled curse, then Evie's voice saying, "I found the trap, and sprang it like you said." Then, taking in the situation with amazing presence of mind, she raised the catch pole, taking a mighty swipe at my attacker, knocking him off balance. He hit the ground.

But it wouldn't take long for him to recover.

I could hear Watson shaking her collar. Whatever had hit her had only winded her temporarily. I got to my feet, grabbed her leash, and the three of us started running like blazes back to the highway, tripping and sloshing through cordgrass and pickleweed, stopping only long enough to retrieve a bewildered Chamois from the disabled station wagon.

Evie complained as we went. "Really, Dee, (puff) you are the absolute limit (puff). I could have really clobbered him if you hadn't dropped the bloody torch."

She explained later that she had observed the attacker enter the bunker and had come upon the scene prepared to do battle.

Thus we reached the relative safety of the highway.

"We'll have to take Shank's pony back to town," I said.

"Haven't heard that expression since we left England," said Evie, as we began to walk.

At first we were apprehensive that our attacker would follow us. But the few cars that passed us were not inclined to stop for a pair of crazy-looking ladies such as we must appear.

Eventually, though, a car did pull up alongside.

"Evening, ladies." A welcome and familiar Texas drawl hailed us. "Going my way?"

I don't know who was more surprised, us or Howard.

With him asking questions like what in the world we thought we were doing, and Evie saying something pithy about Delilah losing her mind, we climbed into the back of the Jaguar, quite done in by the experience.

Along with the tremendous relief that we were safe came the slightly uncharitable thought that now Evie would be able to go back to the Beverly Bay Club with Howard, sparing me the need for entertaining, never mind the inevitable lecture.

In fact, she was mercifully silent all the way home saying only as they dropped me off, "Really, Dee, I had hoped you'd do something with your hair while I was gone. If you will go around looking like the wild woman from Borneo, it's no wonder you have trouble attracting a really nice man."

I devoutly wished I'd had a mirror to offer her.

•　•　•

THE HOUSE SEEMED unusually cold and draughty, until I remembered the broken window. Thank goodness Bud Hefner had helped me to board it up.

Maybe he could help me with another matter. I would have to tell someone about Watson digging up the grave. Hefner, with his historical society connections, would no doubt know the best person to speak to. I would ring him in the morning.

Though much might be said for the restorative powers of tea after such an adventure, that night I felt something a little stronger was called for. I settled on a glass of sherry. Harvey's Bristol Cream takes a bit of beating on a cold winter's night, as long as it's not served over ice—a nasty heathen habit unfortunately prevalent in California.

As I sipped the syrupy liquid, I recalled that Roger had once said my eyes were the same colour as Harvey's. Dear Roger. How I missed him.

Too tired to take myself to bed, I snuggled into my candlewick robe, switched on the electric heater, and curled up on the couch, tucking a rather garish hand-knit afghan (another gift from great-aunt Nell) around my legs. Watson settled down as close to the heater as she dared.

The last thing I noticed as I fell asleep was that the telephone answering machine was signalling several messages. Too late now. They could wait until morning.

It might have made all the difference if I had attended to them straightaway.

22

The Cove

I AWOKE LATE, stiff and uncomfortable from my night on the couch. The room was stuffy and overheated, the air redolent of the smell of damp dog.

My mouth felt like the bottom of a birdcage, and a scratchy throat heralded a cold. No surprise there. After my night on the marsh, I was lucky that's all I came home with. I didn't think it was the flu. I'd had a vaccination a month or so earlier, courtesy of the latest California contribution to a more mobile society, the drive-through flu shot at the local hospital.

A cup of tea was what I needed. I dragged myself to the kitchen and plugged in the electric kettle, passing the time while waiting for it to boil by perusing the morning newspaper. After two cups of the steaming-hot amber liquid had made its way into my system, I began to feel human again and turned my attention to my telephone messages.

The first was from the Puli's owner.

"Do you have anything to report on Mariah?" she asked plaintively. *"We miss her so much. Please let*

me know if there's anything else we can do."

Other than check shelters and place classified ads, I am afraid I had been quite remiss in my efforts on behalf of the absent Mariah. Granted, the events of the past few days had kept me distracted, but that was no excuse for neglecting my clients. I resolved to dedicate the day to Mariah.

The next call gave me the opportunity to direct my anger at someone other than myself.

"I need to find a home for my pet pig," the man said. *"They told me he was a pot-bellied miniature when I got him, but he now weighs over two hundred pounds, and the neighbours are complaining. Can you tell me what to do?"*

Another unfortunate animal had outgrown its novelty value. The pot-bellied pig had yielded to the more manageable pocket pet. Ferrets were the current favourite.

As with too many of the so-called exotic pets, when, inevitably, pot-bellied pigs grow too large, develop unpleasant habits, run afoul of zoning laws, or require expensive specialized veterinary care, their owners express surprise that no one seems willing to take them off their hands.

"Why can't people stick to dogs and cats?" I said to Watson. "If they want to keep pigs, they should go and live on a farm."

Watson gazed at me with what I understood to be complete agreement. She took such rantings in stride, supremely confident they were not directed at her.

"I'll put him in touch with Little Orphan Hammies," I said, continuing to think aloud to Watson. "If they can't take it, the big little pig will be pound bound."

I swear Watson winced.

Beep

"I seen your ad in the paper for the lost Puli."

My cold seemed to have affected my hearing. My ears felt like they were made of flannel. Even so, the man's voice sounded muffled, as if the mouthpiece was covered in an attempt at disguise. *"I want the reward the other woman promised. I'll be at the bark park tomorrow morning, ten 'til noon."* The voice hesitated, then, *"Don't call the cops or the dog's dead."*

What other woman? I looked at the clock. Eleven-fifteen already! I'd have to hurry if I hoped to catch him, especially as I'd have to walk. The station wagon was still out on the wetlands, no doubt giving rise to all kinds of speculation by early morning bird-watchers. I would have to trust to luck that it wouldn't be towed away before I had time to call the auto club.

I showered and dressed. Jeans, a pink lambswool sweater. Tennis shoes, ready for a fast getaway this time. Looking in the mirror, I could see no trace of Amber's handiwork. Two hours of torture wasted.

I SAW THE black Volkswagen as soon as I walked across the parking lot.

A short, skinny individual who had been leaning

against the car flicked away a cigarette and started toward me. I wondered how he knew it was me until I remembered that he had been following me for the past week.

He was dressed in threadbare jeans and a soiled white tee shirt. His cheap rubber thongs did nothing to protect his feet, filthy from walking through the muddy park. He was quite young, mid-twenties I guessed, unhealthy looking, with a face the colour of porridge. His dishwater blond hair was rubber-banded in a stringy ponytail.

I wasn't quite sure how to handle this. The man was a dognapper, quite likely ''a nasty piece of work'', as Tony might say. But though he glanced around warily, as if half-expecting the police to appear, he didn't look dangerous. Actually, he looked more scared than anything. Shivering in the damp air, he wore no jacket; he had nowhere to hide a weapon.

Nothing that Watson and I can't handle, I decided, taking the offensive.

I stretched myself to my full five-foot-one-inch height and said, ''Now, what's all this about the Puli?''

Taken aback, maybe by my manner, he turned his attention to Watson who, ears erect, was doing her best to look menacing.

''That dog bite?'' he asked.

''Only when provoked,'' I said, adding, ''and it doesn't take much. Now, I don't have time to stand here all day. Where's the dog?''

"What about the reward she promised?"

"She?"

"The woman that took the dog from me. Mrs. Redpath."

Mabel had had the dog! Now, this was news.

"You'd better tell me the whole story," I said.

"Well, I found this dog. I knew it was a Puli. My uncle used to have one. It was real friendly, and I guessed somebody would give a reward to get it back, so I took it home and put one of those free found ads in the local paper. Mrs. Redpath answered it. I met her here, and she took the dog, said she'd give me the reward later. Said she didn't have her wallet with her. There was a lot of people around, and she'd said she'd make a scene if I didn't let her have the dog right then. Said to meet her here the next day for the reward."

"And did you meet her?"

"No, she never showed."

I wondered if this was the "cove" Tony had told me about. If so, he was lucky to make beer money. What an incompetent twerp. Doubtless his life was made up of ill-conceived plans like this. I wondered if his mother knew what he did for a living. Mabel would have had no intention of giving him a reward, I was sure. I smiled at the thought of her bullying him out of the dog.

"You said you knew where the dog was."

"What about the reward?" he persisted, scowling.

"That is quite out of the question."

He took a step toward me, close enough that I could smell his stale breath. "Listen you—"

Watson growled a warning, and he stepped back.

Emboldened, I went on. "Don't you threaten me, young man. Now, look here. You may not be aware of it, but Mrs. Redpath was murdered two nights ago."

"Yes, I heard," he said sullenly. "That's why . . ."

"The police are still looking for the killer," I went on impatiently. "If you know what's good for you, you'll forget all about the reward, and just tell me where the dog is, before I inform the police that you've had dealings with a murder victim."

"All right, all right." He was obviously scared now. "I been trying to tell you. I saw your ad in the paper. I tried to call you, but you were never home, and I didn't want to leave a message. I saw you here with Mrs. Redpath the other day, then I saw your car outside the vet's one time, and I followed you home. I wanted to speak to you, but someone showed up at your house, and I left."

He unfolded a pack of cigarettes from his shirt sleeve, took a book of matches from his jeans pocket, and struck one, cupping the flame away from the breeze. Then he went on.

"After I heard the old lady'd been killed, I went to her house to get the dog back. I thought it would be there by itself, and I could just take it. Figured if I couldn't get the reward, I could always sell it to the labs."

Now I was angry. "That's illegal," I said. "A reputable lab wouldn't touch stolen property."

He shrugged. "Some will."

It was no use standing here arguing the toss over that. "Then what happened?" I asked.

"The dog was gone, but you were there."

"So it was you who pushed me and took the newspaper clipping?"

"I thought it was the lost and found ad, and that the cops would trace it to me. That's why I took it. But it was just some old clipping from years ago."

I knew where his ad was. Still in my jacket where I had stashed it after I took it from Mabel's pocket. Well, that explained that. But I was still no closer to the Puli.

"What did the dog look like?" I asked.

"Typical Puli. Dreadlocks. Shaggy black sucker."

It had to be Mariah. In all the recent carryings on, I had forgotten one of my own most important tenets. That after a week or two of wandering, even the best-groomed purebred can look like a shaggy mongrel. That's why many shelters don't allow strays to be groomed. It could make them unrecognizable to their owners. Mabel's words came back to me. "Letting her get in that state. They don't deserve to get her back," she'd said. Was it possible she hadn't recognized the purebred, mistaking the Puli with the hanging mats for a neglected, mixed-breed cockerpoo?

But where was Mariah now? I could guess, but I'd

better find out for sure before I raised the owner's hopes. I turned for home.

The young man made one last effort to salvage his plan.

"Hey. What about the reward?"

"Forget it. Think yourself lucky I don't call the police."

Walking home, I shivered in the chill wind as it occurred to me that I may have just had a narrow escape. Maybe the two murders were not connected after all, and the dognapper had killed Mabel.

Too late, I realized I had forgotten to ask his name. I did, however, have the presence of mind to jot down the Volkswagen's registration number.

As soon as I got home, I dialled the shelter's number, hoping that Rita, the office manager, would be there. She was an old friend and wouldn't hesitate to give me the information I needed. I prayed that no disposition had yet been made on Mabel's pets.

Rita's assistant told me that she was out in the kennel. I left a message for her to call me back as soon as possible.

I was about to call the auto club to see about getting my car towed when I heard a knock on the door. Watson was on her feet and at the door ahead of me.

"If that little twerp's still after the reward, I swear I will call the police this time," I told her.

"Who is it?" I called through the door.

There was no answer. Grabbing Watson by the collar, ready to release her if necessary, I flung the door wide open.

Rosemary Jackson fell across the threshold.

· 23 ·

She's Back

THERE WAS A nasty gash on her forehead, and her greyish blonde hair, usually smoothed into an impeccable French twist, was now dishevelled and matted with blood, some of which had made its way down her left cheek. She was barely conscious.

First making sure that no bones were broken, I lifted her into a sitting position against the wall. Not easy, considering her five-foot-eight-inch, ten-stone frame. I fetched water and a damp towel and started to dab her head and face.

She opened her eyes. "Delilah," she murmured weakly.

"Thank heavens you're all right," I said, though "all right" was relative. "What happened? Have you been in an accident?"

"He tried to kill me." Her voice was so faint I could barely hear her.

"Who? Why? I'm going to ring the police."

"No, please, they'll take me away. I have to talk to you first, to warn you."

"How did you get here? Why didn't you ring 911?"

"I was too scared to stay in the house."

She wasn't making any sense, but first things first.

"Not another word until you're more comfortable," I said. "Can you make it to the sitting-room?"

With my help she managed to get to her feet and, leaning heavily on my shoulder, made her way slowly to the couch.

"Now, let me make you a nice cup of tea, and you can tell me what happened. Though I must say I would rather call the police and an ambulance first."

"No. Not the police. They think I killed Bill." The tears began to trickle down her poor swollen face. I noticed that she was wearing the smart tweed pantsuit she always wore for travel, and I realized with horror that she must have returned from Europe only within the last few hours.

"My dear, I'm so sorry," I said.

"I have to tell you something. The police won't believe me. They think I did it. I have to explain to you, you must finish it for me."

"Finish? Finish what?"

"Please, just listen. I don't know how much longer I can hold out." She closed her eyes, and for a moment I thought she was going to pass out again. Then her eyes opened and she went on, "Do you remember I told you about my sister Valerie, how she disappeared years ago, and how we tried, and tried, but could never find any trace of her?"

"Yes, dear. I remember."

"Well, Bill and I always suspected foul play. It just wasn't like her to take off like that and not leave word. I've been doing my own investigating on and off over the years. Then, just recently, a newspaper friend of mine in Paris told me that the authorities over there had just released some documents that had been sealed for fifty years, since the end of the war. So I went to Paris. With my friend's help I was able to confirm my suspicions."

I fetched the tea and held the cup to her lips. She took a couple of sips, and then I placed the cup and saucer on the end table.

"Bill knew about all this, of course?"

She nodded and closed her eyes again as if to close out the pain of his unexpected death.

"Valerie?" I encouraged.

"I don't think I ever told you she was engaged to Bud Hefner. It was a whirlwind wartime romance. Bill and I were living in Oregon at the time, and had never met him, but she had written us all about him and sent us pictures."

"Yes," I interrupted, trying to spare her unnecessary explanation. "I was reading about their engagement in an old newspaper just recently."

"Well, I was always puzzled by, by . . ." her eyelids fluttered, and she started to drift off again. I gently lifted her legs onto the couch, placed a pillow under her head, and tiptoed out to the kitchen to call the police.

• • •

DETECTIVE MALLORY STOOD in my sitting-room, hands thrust in pockets, apparently deep in thought.

As usual, he was smartly dressed. Today it was a dark grey suit, blue shirt, darker blue tie. Really, he was almost handsome.

I was acutely aware of the mess I must look. Old sweater and jeans, hair getting wilder by the minute, red-eyed, and runny-nosed.

He looked up.

"Now, Mrs. Doolittle. Suppose you tell me exactly what's going on. And don't leave anything out."

His face was serious, displaying none of the barely concealed personal interest of our last encounter in this room.

Rosemary had been taken to the jail ward of St. Mary's Hospital. I was extremely upset that she was in police custody, but was nevertheless relieved that she would receive the care and protection she so obviously needed, though protection from whom I wasn't yet prepared to give utterance to.

Striving to maintain a modicum of dignity, I replied in my most formal manner, "I can add very little to what you already know. Rosemary arrived here about an hour ago, gravely injured. She said someone had tried to kill her."

"She didn't say who?"

"No. You saw her. She was barely conscious. She said she had to warn me about something, and that she wanted me to finish what she had started." In a feeble effort to tidy up the place, I moved Rosemary's tea things from the end table to the sideboard, then continued, ''Won't you please sit down?''

He took the easy chair by the fireplace, where the electric heater burned on low. I pushed Watson to one end of the couch on which she had taken a central position to keep a firm eye on Mallory, having apparently taken an objection to his tone, and sat down myself.

''What was it she wanted you to finish?''

''Something to do with her sister Valerie. She disappeared years ago, you know. Apparently Rosemary has been searching for answers. That's why she went to Paris. She also told me about her sister's engagement to Bud Hefner. But I knew that already from the news clipping I found at Mabel Redpath's house yester—'' the word was out before I considered what I was saying.

''Overlooking for the moment the fact that you were trespassing on a police scene, where's the news clipping now?''

''The dognapper snatched it out of my hand.''

He sighed. ''I knew it wouldn't be long before the subject turned to dogs, Mrs. Doolittle. What dognapper?''

''The one who stole the Puli. At least, I think it was the Puli.''

''A Puli?'' he asked. ''What's a Puli?''

I felt slightly hysterical, as if he was the straight

man in an old music hall comedy team, and I had to
come up with the punch line.

I pulled myself together and described the missing
Mariah.

"What's this dognapper's name?"

"I don't know." How stupid of me not to ask. "He
drives a black Volkswagen, though," I added lamely.

"That narrows it down considerably," he said.
"And why would he take the news clipping from
you?"

"He thought it had to do with the dog he was holding for ransom. And he was after Mabel for the reward."

"It was Mrs. Redpath's dog?"

"No, but she had taken it from him. He was to
meet her in the bark park to get the reward the day
she was killed. When she didn't show up, he went to
her house."

"How do you know all this?"

"He told me."

"Why didn't you report this before?"

He really was the most trying man. "If you recall,"
I answered tartly, "you have reminded me on more
than one occasion that lost dogs are none of your
concern."

He stared hard at the toes of his shoes, as if choosing his next words very carefully.

"You realize, of course, that you've been with-
holding important evidence in a homicide investigation." He looked stern. "This dognapper might very

well turn out to be a suspect in Mrs. Redpath's murder.''

"The same thing had occurred to me," I answered. "He had a motive, the reward, and the opportunity, too. He told me he was at the park about the time she was killed. Maybe he killed Bill Jackson, too, though I can't imagine why."

He was about to respond when the telephone rang.

Explaining that I was expecting an important call, I was off to the kitchen to answer the phone before he had a chance to protest.

It was Rita from the shelter. Yes, she said. Mabel's pets (eight dogs and she wasn't sure exactly how many cats) were still in custody, awaiting further word from her attorney. He had already obtained a "stay of execution" for them pending the settling of the estate. So Mariah, if indeed it was she, was secure for the time being.

Before returning to the sitting-room, I put in a quick call to Mariah's owner, leaving a message suggesting she go to the shelter and have a look at Mabel's dogs to see if she could identify the Puli.

I returned to find Mallory surveying the boarded-up window.

"What happened?" he asked.

"The cat—oh, you wouldn't be interested. Suffice it to say a cat broke the window. Fortunately, Bud Hefner was here at the time, and he helped me."

"What was Hefner doing here?"

Tiresome man. My social life, such as it was, was

really none of his business. Candour gave way to ci-
vility as I replied stiffly, "He came to warn me to
stay away from the bunker. Someone was setting
traps, and he was concerned I might get hurt."

"When was that? About what time?"

Did it matter? "The day before yesterday. Around
four o'clock."

He jotted something in his notebook, then changed
the subject.

"To get back to your dognapper. Why would he
kill Jackson?"

"You're the detective, not I," I retorted, with un-
common waspishness.

"Yes, I am, and I'd appreciate it if you'd keep that
in mind the next time you're tempted to meddle in a
police investigation."

Thus chastised, I tried to redeem myself. "He
could be the man who's been setting traps out in the
wetlands."

"Why would he be setting traps?"

"You'd have to ask him. But he obviously doesn't
like animals. He would have sold the Puli to a re-
search lab if Mabel hadn't taken it from him. Maybe
he killed Jackson because he caught him setting the
traps. I'm sure Bill didn't authorize them. His office
has no record."

Mallory considered this. "Even if he was caught
setting traps, that's hardly enough to justify murder."
He paused, then went on, "How do you know it was
a man?"

"It was very definitely a man who attacked my friend Mrs. Cavendish and me at the bunker last night."

"What? What were you doing out there?"

"I saw a light, and thought maybe someone was setting traps again. So I went over to investigate."

"At night? Alone?"

"I wasn't alone. Mrs. Cavendish and Watson were with me."

He raised his eyebrows. "And what happened?"

I told him how Watson had dug up the skeleton, which I had assumed to be from the Indian burial ground.

Watson stared fixedly at him as if in verification of my story.

"I was still trying to figure it out, when someone hit me from behind. Then Hobo, the cat I was telling you about, jumped on him, and Evie—Mrs. Cavendish—hit him with a catch pole. The man, not the cat," I finished.

Beyond looking at me in mild astonishment, Mallory rather wisely made no comment, and I continued. "We ran out of there as fast as we could. My car's still out there, stuck in the mud," I added, as if proof were needed of our exploits.

"Mrs. Doolittle." Mallory spoke slowly and deliberately. "Please do not meet with this so-called dognapper again, or with anyone else who acts in a suspicious manner, without informing me. You are going to get seriously hurt if you keep interfering in police matters in this way. And stay away from the bunker. I'll send a team over there to investigate the skeleton you claim to have unearthed.''

I'd had it with his patronising manner.

"There's no point in bullying me, Detective Mallory," I said. "I don't see how any of my activities could possibly affect your investigation. I have simply been looking for a lost dog and trying to put a stop to the setting of cruel and vicious traps.''

I was running a fever and it was making me irritable. I just wished he'd leave.

He must have read my mind. He got to his feet, closed his notebook, and said, "I'll let you get some rest. Oh, one last thing, I don't suppose there's a chance you got the Volkswagen's license number?''

With modest triumph, I produced the required number from my jeans pocket.

I saw him to the door, closing it behind him with almost unseemly haste. The phone was ringing again.

◦ 24 ◦

Taking a Stand

IT WAS PERHAPS with more bravado than good sense that I set out on foot the next morning for my rendezvous with the nameless caller.

At last, sunshine. "No smog in the basin," the television weather wag had said. A cool breeze had blown away the storm clouds, leaving only puffy white cumuli for contrast in an otherwise stunningly blue sky. It was one of those mornings where you could see, if not quite forever, then certainly as far as Santa Catalina Island, twenty-six miles away.

Looking inland, the San Gabriel Mountains were clearly visible, their peaks covered with snow. It was time for the annual newspaper feature illustrating how one could surf and ski the same day, riding the waves in the morning, then after only a two-hour drive, ski in the afternoon. If one had the energy.

Perfect weather, in my opinion, though some locals might consider it cold. Things were drying out after the storm, and steam rose from the rain-soaked redwood fences that lined the gardens in my neighbourhood. A lovely time of day, so peaceful this early in the morning. The only sounds were the squabbling of birds in the hibiscus and the increasingly loud rush of the surf as I neared the beach.

I HAD BEEN surprised to hear from the dognapper again. His voice, though still obviously disguised, had sounded different. But that was probably because my ears were no longer stuffed up from the head cold.

"It's about the dog you're looking for," he had said.

"Yes," I started to say, "I'm following up on that." But he had interrupted, saying hastily, "Meet me at the end of the pier, tomorrow morning, seven a.m. I can get the dog back for you."

He had hung up before I could ask why he hadn't seen fit to share this information earlier.

I had called Mariah's owner again, to get her to hold off going to the shelter until I had checked out this new lead, but there was no reply.

This morning, my head clearer after a decent night's sleep, I was having second thoughts about this meeting. Mallory's warning came back to me. He might well be right. The evidence pointed to a strong possibility that the dognapper could be Mabel's killer. I certainly would be more cautious than I had been when I met him in the park the previous day.

This feeling of unease had been reinforced by the realization that Watson would have to stay home. She was already on her feet looking eagerly at her leash hanging by the kitchen door, when I remembered.

"Sorry, luv. Not today," I told her. "You're not allowed on the pier."

I considered calling Mallory but he would tell me not to go. Besides, any sign of the police would scare off the dognapper. Getting Mariah back was my priority.

I dialled Tony's number, hoping he could come with me, but there was no reply. He was probably at the beach already. But on the chance that he was still in bed, or out walking Trixie, I left a message.

There were always people on the pier, I reassured myself. Surfers, lifeguards, fishermen. I'd be all right as long as I kept my wits about me.

There were indeed plenty of people about, but most of them were gathering on the beach, their attention focused on the rally. I was surprised not to see Tony among the wet suits and surfboards ranged sentrylike along the beach preparing to make their Stand in the Sand.

Dr. Willie had chosen a good day for the event. The storms seemed to be over for the time being, though heavy swells rolling in from the South Pacific hinted at more rain to come.

Everyone was out to enjoy the spectacle and the sunshine. I made my way along the bike path, dodging the cyclists, skateboarders, and Rollerbladers. No one seemed to want to walk anywhere anymore. If they couldn't drive their cars, they attached wheels to their feet. Rollerbladers pushed strollers carrying in-

fants destined to grow up believing that wheels were
the only means of transportation.

In a roped-off VIP section on the cliffs overlooking
the beach, the mayor, city council members, Costa
Bella executives, and members of the Coastal Commission, Evie and Howard among them, were gathered.

The pier-side parking lot was full, but I could see
no sign of the Volkswagen. Hardly surprising, given
the crowds. It was quite likely the dognapper had had
to park some distance away.

I climbed the steps from the bike path and walked
the length of the deserted pier. It was too early for
Roxie's, a favourite 1940's-style diner, to be open.
The bait and tackle shop had a Gone Fishin' sign in
the window. Even the lifeguard tower appeared to be
empty, its occupants no doubt taking part in the rally.

Only the seagulls remained. Usurped from their
customary early-morning stake-out on the beach, they
perched on the pier railings, turned as one eastwards
to catch the early-morning rays, their white plumage
rosy from the reflected sunrise. A sudden breeze ruffled their feathers. I shivered, too. It was always
cooler out on the pier, more exposed as it was to the
elements. I was glad I had worn my dark green
hooded sweatshirt and pants.

Even from a distance I could see that the one solitary figure at the end of the pier wasn't the dognapper. Height, bearing, and manner of dress announced

the identity before I was close enough to recognize the person.

Bud Hefner came toward me, hand outstretched in greeting.

"Good morning, Mrs. Doolittle. A lovely morning for the rally, is it not?" I was struck again by the formality of his speech, so un–southern Californian. He grasped the brim of his homburg hat as the wind caught at it.

I could scarcely hide my surprise at seeing him here. He looked so out of place. One expects shorts and tee shirts, sandals and wet suits on the pier, not three-piece suits and homburg hats.

But I was glad to see him. He would offer protection, if needed. And I would have someone to chat with while I waited. Here was an opportunity to ask him about the skeleton that Watson had unearthed in the bunker.

We stood watching the activity on the beach for a minute or two. Then I broached the subject.

"This is most fortuitous, meeting you like this," I began. "I know you and the historical society have an interest in the bunker out on the wetlands. I need to ask your advice about something."

Even though he was still holding on to the brim of his hat, partially covering his face, I could see him start at the mention of the bunker.

But his voice conveyed no surprise.

"Really? What was that?" he asked.

"I have to confess to feeling a little embarrassed

telling you about this," I said, "especially after your advice to stay away from the bunker. Which, I'm ashamed to say, I ignored. Be that as it may, when I was there the other evening, Watson, my dog, started digging, and I'm rather afraid she unearthed a skeleton. It's no doubt part of the Indian burial ground that's said to be in the vicinity. I feel I should own up to someone, and I was hoping you could advise me as to whom."

My confession was met with silence.

I don't know what kind of response I expected. Outrage, perhaps, that I would allow my dog to desecrate holy ground? Disgust that I would ignore his advice?

Finally, his voice stiff with anger, he said, "What game are you trying to play?"

As he spoke, the breeze lifted his hat right off his head and sent it bowling along on its brim, under the railing and out to sea to join other flotsam and jetsam for time and tide to play with.

We both followed it with our eyes. Then, turning back to continue the conversation, which had taken a very peculiar turn, I noted with growing fear and dawning realization that his grievously disfigured face bore a fresh scar. Several deep red scratches ran across his left brow and cheek. The kind of scratch that an angry cat might inflict.

♣ 25 ♣
Choices

As USUAL, I had been jumping to all the wrong conclusions. Suspecting everyone but the real culprit. But Hobo's scratches left no doubt as to who had attacked me in the bunker.

I looked around for help. Not a soul was within hailing distance. I could see Lily Semple pushing her father in a wheel-chair along the bike path. (At least she wasn't on Rollerblades.) On the cliffs I could just make out Evie in a bright red outfit and matching straw hat. The Stand in the Sand grew longer as more people arrived. They were all like actors on a stage, and my seat was up in the gods.

With outward calm and inward trepidation I said, "Game? I don't understand what you mean."

A squadron of pelicans flew sedately by the end of the pier. In contrast to their graceful, rhythmic flight, a helicopter hovered noisily overhead, probably monitoring the rally. Disturbed, the seagulls had left their railing perches, swooping and shrieking in annoyance. Their cries, the helicopter, and the waves crashing against the pier pilings would drown out any calls I might have made for help.

Far below, a solitary surfer, black wet suit silhouetted against the morning sky, braved the heavy swells, sitting astride his board waiting for the next set. I waved for help. He returned a friendly greeting.

I remembered the dognapper. He should be here soon. My mouth dry with fear, I managed to say, "I didn't tell you the reason I'm here. Actually, I'm meeting someone. He should be here any minute." Desperately I looked back down the pier for the twerp, now suddenly transformed into saviour. But the only other person on the pier was a fisherman concentrating on casting his line into the ocean.

Hefner's smile, that same odd, crooked smile that I had once thought strangely attractive, now offered only menace.

"I'm the one who called you," he said.

"You? What do you know about the dog?"

"You told me about it, remember? A simple ruse." He turned up the collar of his overcoat against the breeze, then continued. "You're getting too close to the truth, Mrs. Doolittle. I know Rosemary Jackson came to see you. It won't be long before you and the police figure it all out. It's time to end the charade."

"*You* attacked Rosemary? I don't understand."

"It's a long, sad story, Mrs. Doolittle. A story of a young man desperate to save his skin."

He looked toward the beach where the rally was in full swing. The crowds waving, presumably clapping and cheering, though it was impossible to hear from this distance, as Dr. Willie addressed them.

"There is no hurry. Everyone is busy with their foolish rally. Perhaps I do owe you an explanation."

His real name was Hans Dieter, he began. As a German soldier during World War II, he had been stationed at a prisoner of war camp. His war injuries had prevented him from being returned to active duty, and he had been assigned guard duty in the hospital ward.

It was there that he met the dying Bud Hefner. During those final days of the war, captor and captive, two young men who might at another time and place have become friends, had shared confidences and talked about their backgrounds. Neither had any family. For Hefner there was only Valerie, a young girl to whom, in a typical whirlwind wartime romance, he had become engaged after a very brief acquaintance.

When Hefner died, Dieter had seized the opportunity to escape capture by the advancing Allies by assuming the dead man's identity. They were of similar colouring and build, and Dieter, like many Europeans, spoke fluent English. Young and desperate to escape, he had not given much thought to the consequences of his actions, and in the chaotic days at the end of the war, it had not been difficult to deceive the authorities.

"Of course," he said, gently rubbing his scarred face with the side of his index finger, "this is what made it possible."

That was what had been nagging at me ever since my visit to the beauty parlour. As a veteran, Hefner would have been entitled to reconstructive surgery; in the aftermath of World War II, great advances had been made in that field. I had wondered why he hadn't taken advantage of that. Now the reason was all too painfully clear.

From the beach came a faint crackle of applause as the rally proceeded. There must be musicians there, too; every so often a few notes of music would reach my ears. I wished I could turn around and watch.

But all my attention was concentrated on the man before me. He was dangerous, and I had to be alert to his every move. For now, though, he seemed content to talk.

He knew he was taking a big risk in attempting to deceive Valerie, he continued, but he counted on the fact that she and Hefner had only known each other for a very brief time. After four years apart, the hope was that she would put any perceived changes down to dimmed memory and his disfigurement.

He had intended to remain in California only long enough to establish his identity and break off the engagement to Valerie. But the city had hailed him as a hero, many business opportunities had opened up to him, and he was persuaded to stay. And at first, Valerie had appeared to accept him.

Up to that point, I could have pitied him. He had harmed nobody but himself, doomed to live a life of deceit. One brief moment of decision and the course of life can be changed forever.

But before long, Valerie had discovered the deception.

The tone of his voice changed now, as if he, too, recognized that a certain line had been crossed. "I was reluctantly obliged to kill her," he said quietly.

"I buried her at the bunker," he continued. He had fabricated a story about how he and Valerie had argued, and she had run away. The police had questioned him at length, but the case had eventually been dropped for lack of evidence, or, indeed, a corpus delecti. Valerie became just another missing person, eventually forgotten by everyone.

Except the Jacksons.

"I might have got away with it if they hadn't moved to Surf City a year or so later. But they would never let the matter rest," he said. Rosemary, in particular, had questioned him repeatedly over the years.

"Recently, her attitude had turned from curiosity to suspicion. She would ask questions about my childhood here and my years in the service. I knew she was getting close to the truth."

He had gone to her house that morning to try to convince her otherwise, but she had already left for Europe. Bill was there, and he had confronted him with their suspicions, telling him why Rosemary had gone to Paris.

"I had to kill him then, you understand. It was not planned. I meant just to threaten him. I picked up a kitchen knife. It was all over in a few seconds,'' he said simply.

He still had Rosemary to deal with. He had watched her house, waiting for her return.

"You almost killed her, too," I said accusingly.

"A mistake," he said. "I thought she was dead. I heard someone coming, and I had to leave before I was sure."

Once Costa Bella announced their plans to develop the wetlands property, he needed time to dispose of any evidence that might remain after almost fifty years. He had set the traps to scare off both people and the wild animals that had recently begun to disturb the area.

"Then it *was* you at the bunker that night," I said.

"I tried to warn you." He shrugged.

When the historical society began lobbying to preserve the bunker as a monument, he had seen it as an opportunity to keep the site undisturbed and had joined their efforts.

"But enough talking, Mrs. Doolittle. The rally is nearly over. People will be coming up on the pier soon. Time to bring our little chat to a close."

It was the first time I'd seen a gun close up.

"It's time to end the charade," he said once more. "It's hard to live a lie."

Out of the corner of my eye, I could see that the fisherman had gathered his tackle together and was heading in our direction.

"Wait," I said, playing for time. "What about Mabel?"

"Mabel?"

"The woman in the park," I said. "Did you kill her, too?"

"How astute you are, Mrs. Doolittle. You're wasting your talents looking for lost animals," he said with a twisted smile. "Mabel. Foolish woman. So curious. Like those cats of hers. Isn't that what they say, 'curiosity killed the cat'? She discovered me setting the traps one evening when she was tending her charges. I had no choice."

"You've had plenty of choices," I said. "You just made the wrong ones."

"Well, this is the last one I'll have to make," he said, raising the gun.

The helicopter was flying so low, I could barely hear what he was saying. Someone was addressing us with a bullhorn. But like PA systems the world over, it was totally unintelligible.

The fisherman was running now, but I couldn't wait.

The helicopter had provided a distraction. Catching Hefner/Dieter off guard, I gave him a push. We struggled for a moment, but he had the advantage of weight and height and shoved me hard against the railing. I lost my footing and slipped. I heard the gun go off as I fell.

I like to do my swimming in a warm pool, preferably in a fetching swimsuit. Not fully dressed, in the cold briny, with an eight-foot swell. I hit the water and kept going down, a long way down, weighted by heavy shoes and sweats. I looked up to see green bubbles above my head. I came to the surface, buffeted and pummeled by the heavy swell, then sank again. I remembered something about you come up three times. "I'm going to drown," I thought with certainty. "I hope someone will take care of Watson."

Gulping saltwater, I surfaced a second time.

"'Allo, Mrs. D. What's all this then? It's a bloomin' fine time to be taking a dip," said Tiptoe Tony as he pulled me onto his surfboard.

♣ 26 ♣

Connecting the Dots

I LAY ACROSS the board like an overdressed flounder, and with Tony swimming and guiding, the waves carried us in to the beach. People splashed out to help us as we waded the last few yards ashore.

A crowd had gathered. Someone threw a blanket around my shoulders. I sat down on the sand, trying to regain my breath and my composure, circled by curious onlookers.

"What happened?" asked one.

"Some lady fell off the pier, man."

"Bummer."

"Now then, lads, clear the way," said Tony.

A red jeep screeched to a halt, and a tanned young lifeguard leaped out, prepared to do whatever life-saving procedures were necessary.

Fortunately, none were.

Officer Offley splashed along the shoreline toward us, wet sand clinging to his shiny black boots and the pant legs of his nicely pressed uniform. Detective

Mallory wished to see me immediately, if I was able, he said.

After a quick word with the lifeguard, Offley handed me into the jeep. Tony, giving his board into the custody of a fellow surfer, joined us, uninvited.

Back on the pier, the police had taken over Roxie's Diner as a command post. The young manager stood at the door, officiously waving away the curious.

My squishy tennis shoes left a trail of sandy footprints across the newly washed floor, as Offley escorted me to one of the red vinyl booths. The sun-warmed seat felt good through my damp clothes.

A second blanket fell around my shoulders, and Detective Mallory slipped into the seat opposite.

"Are you all right?" Concern showed on his face. I was too embarrassed to answer. By ignoring Mallory's warnings, I had made a complete fool of myself.

I gazed out of the window. A few yards off the end of the pier, a pod of dolphins frolicked and swam their way north toward Palos Verdes. I almost wished I was back in the water with them.

Mallory spoke again. "Do you feel up to answering a few questions? We won't keep you long. It's important to get details while everything's still fresh in your mind."

Believe me, I thought, it will be a long time before I forget one detail of today's harrowing adventure.

Tony, still in his wet suit, came over to the table with two cups of steaming hot chocolate and sat down, unasked, next to me. My cold hands clutched the hot pottery mug gratefully.

"Now look 'ere mate," said Tony. "She needs to get 'ome out of them wet clothes. You can't keep 'er 'ere."

"It's all right, Tony," I said, finding my voice at last. "Detective Mallory's only doing his job." My teeth chattered as I spoke.

"And a right cock-up he's made of it, too, if you arst me. If he'd been doing it right, you wouldn't be in this two and eight now."

Mallory looked puzzled.

"Two and eight—state. Cockney rhyming slang," I interpreted.

"Good job I was out on me board. Gawd knows what would've 'appened if I 'adn't been there."

"I can swim, Tony," I said defensively.

"Yeah, I noticed," he said sarcastically.

There was a commotion at the door. I looked up to see Evie pushing her way past the protesting Offley, followed by Howard, carrying her gold leather handbag, umbrella, and a brown carryall, which I knew must contain Chamois.

"Do you mind, Constable!" she shrilled. "I have to look after my friend." Then, catching sight of me, "Dee! What on earth . . . ? Someone said you'd been shot."

I assured her that all was well.

"Then why are you sitting here in those wet clothes? Have you been arrested? We'll get you a solicitor at once," she said, totally ignoring Mallory. "Howard, call Max. Demand that Delilah be released immediately."

Mallory regarded her in stunned silence.

Howard reached into his pocket for his cell phone, but I said, "Really, Howard. It's all right. I have to tell Detective Mallory all I know before I go home." Then to Evie, "Evie, please. I've just got to get this over with."

"Very well. We'll wait for you. We will be witnesses, to make sure there's no coercion." She glared at Mallory.

Howard fetched two chairs and placed them at the end of the booth. Evie sat down cautiously, first wiping the spotless seat with a napkin.

Mallory, displaying what I considered superb self-control under the circumstances, allowed them to get settled, then said, "Now, Mrs. Doolittle. What led you to meet with Hefner after I had specifically warned you to stay out of the investigation?"

He was distracted momentarily by a slight scuffling sound coming from Evie's carry-all, which she had placed at her feet, but apparently decided he'd rather not inquire.

Feeling somewhat revived by the hot chocolate, I told him about the anonymous call I had received from someone whom I had assumed to be the dog-napper.

"I thought I had advised you to stay away from him," said Mallory. "But then, when you realized you'd been duped, why didn't you leave?"

"I didn't realize it. You'd said nothing about Hefner being a suspect."

"It wasn't until you told me that Hefner had warned you away from the bunker that I got suspicious," he replied.

"Lucky you tumbled to it when you did," put in Tony.

"But I didn't have much to go on until after I had interviewed Rosemary Jackson," Mallory continued, ignoring him. "That wasn't possible until this morning. By the time I got to the hospital last night, she had been given a sedative."

He waited while the manager placed five cups of coffee on the table, making the simple task last as long as possible in hopes, no doubt, of hearing something worth repeating. Mallory stared him down, and the young man retreated.

"Rosemary was lucky to survive," he went on. "There was no question that Hefner intended to kill her. He may have been interrupted by the arrival of a water delivery truck. There were two new bottles on the front porch. We are bringing the driver in for questioning." He ran his hand through his hair in that familiar gesture of his. "I'm sure he killed Bill Jackson, too. What I've yet to figure out is why."

"I believe I know," I said.

"I sort of thought you might." Mallory smiled encouragingly, and I told the group how Hans Dieter had been passing himself off as Bud Hefner all these years, and why, so long ago, he had thought it necessary to kill Valerie. How Rosemary had never given up on her quest to uncover the truth, her departure for Paris to find the final piece of the puzzle coinciding with Hefner's decision to put an end to her inquiries once and for all.

"Incredible," said Evie, rummaging in her purse from which she produced a packet of Sobranies and a gold cigarette holder.

"Light, sweetie." She waved the holder at Howard.

The manager, never out of hearing, as far as I could tell, appeared. At the same moment, Chamois managed to work the zipper apart and poke his head out of the carryall.

"No smoking. No dogs," announced the manager, apparently enjoying the opportunity to participate in the discussion no matter how peripherally.

"Young man, my friend has done this community a great public service," said Evie. "We cannot let petty rules interfere with important business. Now, be a sweetie and fetch me some matches."

The manager fell back in defeat.

Mallory had sent a team to investigate the skeleton in the bunker. The pathologist's preliminary guess was that it was of fairly recent origin. Certainly not ancient Indian.

"From what you say, this could well be Rosemary's sister," said Mallory. "If you hadn't been so determined to find out who was setting the traps, we might never have solved her disappearance."

I thought that rather generous of him, considering all the trouble I'd caused.

"I had something to do with that, you know," chimed in Evie, determined not to be left out of the limelight.

Ignoring her, Mallory continued. "We sent a patrol car to your house to warn you. When you weren't there but your dog was, we got worried."

It was rather nice to think of being the cause of Mallory's alarm. Though I noticed he played safe and used the royal "we".

"But how did you know where I was?"

"I called Tipton, here, he being the only one of your friends who I thought might know. He said you'd left a message on his machine that you were going to the pier."

"Always glad to lend an 'and to the perlice," said Tony. Turning to me, he said, "I was coming down 'ere anyway to get a bit of surfing in before the rally. You waved to me from the pier, remember? Acourse, I didn't realize you was in trouble, like, 'til you dived in."

"We dispatched the helicopter," continued Mallory, "and had a stake-out on the pier. The fisherman," he explained in response to my raised eyebrows.

"And this dear boy saved your life," said Evie, patting Tony delicately on the shoulder of his still damp wet suit.

Tony looked sheepish.

"How fortunate that you were nearby," she continued. "So brave. How can you endure that cold water? Aren't you afraid of sharks?"

"Nah. Only thing I'm scared of is getting sick from the pollution."

I brought the conversation back to the matter at hand.

"What happened to Bud, er Hans Dieter?" I asked.

Mallory shook his head: "Drowned, probably. We found his pistol on the pier, one bullet expired. Several witnesses saw him fall into the ocean. Not much chance he survived. The Coast Guard and lifeguard boats are out looking for him."

"I felt he intended to kill himself all along," I said, remembering Hefner's haunted look when he said, "It's time to end the charade." I shuddered. "Whether or not I was going to join him as well is something I'd rather not dwell on."

I sneezed. The dousing hadn't done my cold any good. I was getting stiff and suddenly felt overwhelmingly tired.

Evie got to her feet. "I'm sure you've got all you need for now," she said to Mallory. "Delilah's got to get home. If you want any further information, you must call our solicitor. Howard, give the constable Max's number."

Howard removed a business card from a silver case and scribbled a number on the reverse.

Mallory concurred. "Thank you, Mrs. Doolittle,"

he said. "I think anything else can wait until later."

"Just one more thing," I said, trying not to sneeze again. "What about the dognapper?"

"That was a wild goose, or should I say an 'onky webloe' chase, you sent us on, Mrs. Doolittle," he replied with a smile. "We had him in for questioning, but his alibi's watertight. He had a bunch of animals at his place, though. Something you might want to look into when you're feeling better. But he didn't kill Mabel Redpath."

"I know that. Hefner told me he killed Mabel because she'd seen him setting the traps."

Had Mabel also found out about Hefner's assumed identity? We would never know. Neither would we know the true object of the investigation she had sent me on. But I made no mention of that to Detective Mallory. What I had seen as a favour to a fellow Brit, he would undoubtedly consider "interfering in police business."

Sometimes it is as well to know when to keep one's mouth shut.

· 27 ·

The Legacy

"YOU'RE SURE YOU don't want me to stay for a few days?" Evie was all solicitude.

"Really, no. Once I get out of these miserable, wet clothes I'll be fine."

She made us a pot of tea while I showered and changed into my oldest, most comfortable sweats and woollen socks.

"Promise me," she said, as she set out the tea at the kitchen table, "that there will be no more escapades. You could have been killed. You really have to find a different hobby. Looking for lost pets is all very well, but much more hazardous than one might have expected. I'm giving a dinner party at Thanksgiving, and I intend to invite several really nice men."

She turned to her husband, who had just come in from supervising Chamois in the backyard.

"Howard, you can find someone for Delilah, can't you?" It was more a statement than an inquiry.

He threw a conspiratorial grin in my direction. "I

think Delilah's perfectly capable of finding her own beaus," he said.

Before Evie had a chance to elaborate further on the Really Nice Man theme, I changed the subject.

"Howard, I owe you an apology."

He raised his eyebrows in question.

"When I was rummaging around in Mabel's house—the SSCOWL woman, you know—I discovered her last telephone bill. She had indeed been making those threats to you. I was so sure that she wouldn't have done such a thing. Just shows how misguided she was in her zeal to protect the wetlands."

Howard listened with interest, then said magnanimously, "Well, no harm done. The poor woman's dead. Forget it."

"So there'll be no more calls. And no more trapping, either, thank goodness," I said brightening. "But after all the uproar, there's still no conclusion. The battle over the wetlands continues."

"There's no quick solution to that one," he replied gravely. "The outcome will be a compromise, each side thinking that the other's gained the advantage. It's a question of landowners' rights versus those of the original inhabitants."

"And who might they be?" I asked. "Local citizens? Native Americans? Indigenous wildlife?"

Evie, in a tone that indicated she didn't care for the direction the discussion had taken, got to her feet saying, "Well, I can't wait to get home and have a little lie down. I must confess, I feel quite done in by the whole experience. It's all very tiresome. And I, for one, have had enough of Coastal Commission meetings to last me for a very long time.''

I guessed that if Howard planned to continue his career as a commissioner, he would be doing it without the company of his wife.

They departed soon afterward, amid cries of ''Call you soon, sweetie'' and ''We expect you at Thanksgiving. No excuses.'' Evie had given me one last hug, then held me at arm's length saying, ''And sweetie, please try to do something about your hair.''

Considering what I and my hair had been through in the last few hours, I thought this was a bit much.

I watched them drive down the street, turn left at Pacific Coast Highway and, with one last wave, head south for San Diego.

I walked back into the house, Watson at my heels.

''You were right about that Hefner man all along,'' I said, stroking her large brown head.

Watson looked smug.

''And Hobo, the heroic cat, got his revenge, too. I wonder where he is. I'll put some fresh food out on the porch tonight and hope he comes by for a visit.''

I really needed to get him back to Dr. Willie for a re-check, but I doubted if he'd ever trust me and my pet-carrier again.

It was with considerable surprise that, on entering the kitchen, who should I discover with his nose in Watson's water bowl but the heroic cat himself. He must have wandered in while we were waving good-bye to Howard and Evie. Though somewhat bedraggled, the remnants of a very dirty dressing still hanging from his body, he really looked none the worse for wear, all things considered.

Watson wagged her tail in greeting. I, not wanting to scare him off again, tiptoed into the sitting-room, where I looked in dismay at the results of his last abrupt departure: the window, still covered with plywood.

"I suppose I'll have time to get that taken care of now all the excitement is over," I said to Watson.

There was also the station wagon, still out on the wetlands, to be retrieved.

Nothing that couldn't wait until I'd had another cup of tea, I decided.

I poured the tea, then sank gratefully into my comfy old couch, and played back my messages.

Beep

Mallory's call from earlier this morning. I was to contact him immediately. Was I deluding myself, or did his tone of voice suggest something more than official concern?

Beep

Mariah's owner, sounding confused. *"Delilah. I went to the shelter. It's definitely Mariah. She's in terrible shape, though. Someone's shaved off her cords."*

"Wait 'til she finds out she's been spayed," I said to Watson.

"But they won't let me have her because she's been impounded as part of someone's estate," the message continued. *"I don't understand. But the woman in the office said to talk to you about it. She was sure there wouldn't be any problem."*

I was completely stumped as to what that meant.

The next call enlightened me.

Beep

"Mrs. Doolittle. This is Morley Peters, of Peete, Peters, and Peterson, attorneys. Please call me at your earliest convenience to discuss your legacy from the estate of Mrs. Mabel Redpath . . ."

A little nest egg coming my way. How kind. The thought had barely formed, however, before my hopes were dashed. *". . . in consideration of your caring for her pets. They are now being held at the animal shelter, accruing boarding fees, so you need to decide on their disposition as soon as possible."*

He concluded with an astonishing series of numbers—telephone, pager, cell phone, voice mail (home and office), and fax—where he could be reached. Clearly, Morley Peters was a man who left nothing to chance.

Reaching from the grave, Mabel continued to torment me.

The muttley crew was mine.